BURN MY BONSAI

KEVIN FARRAN

KIT PUBLISHING

ISBN : 978-0-986727375
KDP ISBN: 9781718074934
Copyright: Kit Publishing and Kevin Farran
www.kfarranauthor.com

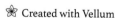 Created with Vellum

Though by no means a Japanophile, the author has expressed his views in fiction from his understandings of what is an immensely deep and varied culture. Particular thanks should be given to the late Ivan Morris whose many works but particularly 'The Nobility of Failure' published by Charles E Tuttle Co., were of outstanding insight and inspiration.

For my family whose tolerance of my endeavours is only ever eclipsed by their positive support for those same madcap endeavours.

BURN MY BONSAI

1

Peter was fourth in line, but wasn't concerned about the wait. He had more than enough time to get to work and it would be a pleasant treat for the old man and himself. The two old grannies in front were obviously excited by the prospect of the succulent red bean paste. They shuffled and dithered like hyperactive lawn gnomes. They lacked the classic pipe but certainly had the odd hat. Watching their excitement, he wondered if his stomach wasn't half the reason he had taken to studying Japanese in the first place. The array of foods and the pride of presentation were far more appealing to him than anything the French could produce. He'd been told the Japanese had a fascination with both the Chinese and French cuisine, largely a result of Hirohito's inclinations, but that didn't persuade Peter in the least. He new where his stomach took him and the taiyaki cakes would be an exceptional way to start his afternoon of gardening. The old woman turned back and smiled up at the gangly blond Scandinavian. She wanted to say something, but was unsure of whether he spoke Japanese. Overcome by the excitement elicited from the fragrance wafting out of the small take-away window, the old woman couldn't help herself. She stretched her wrinkled neck up like an aged stork and the hooded, creased eyes bore into him. She raised her eyebrows and the folds over her eyes receded slightly in a vain attempt to improve her vision. Hundreds of tiny vertical folds like a wispy moustache stood shoulder to shoulder over her top lip. She touched a gnarled finger to her lips and leaned close to him.

"It smells like heaven. These are the best taiyaki in all of Tokyo."

A cackle grumbled from the woman bearing the equally antiquated scowl beside her. "That's not so, Shitamachi has the best."

"Don't mind her, she's an idiot, this is the best."

"No, that's not true. She knows nothing." The woman in the pale blue washbasin type hat was as strident as the other one was wrinkled.

The line shuffled forward a step and it struck Peter as strange, that though they obviously were unsure of his Japanese fluency, the smell coming from the window bridged all hesitancies. He wanted to support the round little bundle, who had first spoken to him, without causing an octogenarian rumble. He could just imagine the clash of wrinkles and gnarled thumbs if the street were to erupt into a bakery slugfest. It would be outrageously un-Japanese. "I think the chestnut paste is the best here but the anko, sweet red beans, are the best at the stall inside Ueno Park."

"Ah so, so." The little bundle was thankful for the support. "That's true isn't it?"

"You don't now Kanedasan," the basin hat quipped. "You'll eat anything."

"If it's taiyaki, yes, probably. But I think the foreigner is right."

"Un." The pale blue washbasin hat nodded and again shuffled closer to the window. She leaned into the jolly little bundle called Kanedasan. "At least the foreigners have an appreciation of Japanese cakes."

"That's so, isn't it?" Kanedasan turned back to him and her smile, scattered with gold caps and black spaces, grinned at him as if he were a new collaborator in the plot to overthrow the blue washbasin hat. "Your Japanese is very good."

"No, no. I speak like a text book." The two women cackled and he saw the sullen young serving girl behind the counter glance at him as if he were gum on her shoe.

The little bundle put a hand on his elbow and leaned toward him as if some great conspiracy were about to be hatched. "You need a Japanese girlfriend to help you. Make you relax with Japanese girl."

"Kanedasan are you still trying to get lucky?" They both cackled again and the round bundle slapped the washbasin's arm.

Peter leaned over the little woman and spoke to the washbasin hat. "We already have matching appetites."

The sprightly bouquet of wrinkles turned hopefully back to the towering blond foreigner. "That's so, isn't it?"

"Yes, but I am sure you are a fantastic cook and would fatten me up so much you wouldn't want me in two months," Peter said. He actually quite liked the cackling old girls.

"Ha! She eats too much of her own cooking as it is. How do you think she got so round? Eh Kanedasan?"

"It's a sculpted stomach," the picket fence of gold caps

receded behind a bristle of wrinkles, "a gourmet's stomach." The rotund old Kanedasan would not be out done.

"You are so full of crap! You say the stupidest things." The serving girl in the window passed the thin brown bag to the two old women. Her perfunctory bow was polite but had the enthusiasm of a dishrag. The octogenarians had bought five pieces of the pancake-like sandwiches. They were no doubt for a tea gathering of battling old hens. They both shoved their noses into the bag and swooned.

The little round Kanedasan glanced up at him and nodded to the brooding twenty-year-old on the other side of the take-away window. "Japanese girl, she will help your learning."

"Of what?" The other grey granny leered winding the coil of the precocious Kanedasan.

"Many things." She cackled suggestively as her friend again slapped her elbow. Her eyes twinkled with an eighty-year-old mischief.

"Come on Kanedasan, you're fishing again."

Kanedasan's years evaporated in a girly giggle that erupted through the decades that had bent her spine, but not her spirit. It made the washbasin seem plain and unin-spiring. "Over to Ueno for anko paste. We will go there next week." They bowed repeatedly and trundled away with their booty. They were an unlikely manzai or comedy, duo he thought.

He watched the two old girls scurry off to meet a giggling mass of grey hairs, where he would no doubt be a topic of conversation. Even in the late nineteen nineties, in a city like Tokyo, interaction with a foreigner was an amuse-ment for older Japanese. He turned back to the glum looking girl behind the counter. She always looked like she had constipation of the heart. She wasn't unattractive and she knew that he spoke Japanese, as he had visited the shop at least twenty times in the month he had been in Tokyo. Impatience like a foul smelling draft glanced from her eyes with her formal, unemotional welcome. He ordered three chestnut Taiyaki cakes and passed a thousand yen note to the girl. She took the note politely, but with an immense lethargy of emotional involvement. Peter couldn't stand the gushiness of Americans, but this girl was the extreme antithesis and could very well pass for a corpse of courtesy. As she flipped the cakes to brown both sides he noticed how the porcelain-like foundation, applied so heavily as makeup in Japan, gave an intensely unwholesome, lifeless air to her already sullen countenance. Her rusty-brown, died hair lacked vibrancy and her tight expression, left him wondering if the two old grannies had it completely wrong. He couldn't possibly learn anything interesting and vibrant from the cadaver in front of him.

She said something to him but it was lost. He couldn't make out a word. The windows of the little shop front shuddered. A scowl of hatred drifted across the young girl's ceramic face, but was quickly washed away by a contemptuous disdain of acceptance. He still struggled with the extreme noise and reached for the bag of treats. His eyes squinted with the sudden change in atmosphere.

The black loudspeakers, like the bellowing mouth of the bowels of hell, thudded sound waves into his rib cage. He almost dropped the treats. The volume was beyond ridiculous and thundered through everything within ten meters. Unfortunately his scooter was parked at the side of the road beside the blaring ultra rightist's van. There were some things one could accept from a foreign culture, but these idiots were one of the hideous aspects of Japan that Peter loathed, in fact most Japanese also found the little puppets

repugnant. The bastards had stopped right beside his bike,
blocking it in. The volume was so loud he wasn't sure he
could actually get close enough to retrieve his scooter. He
took a step toward the line of bikes just as the passenger
sliding door of the van rolled open and four uniformed
rightist fanatics tumbled out. As they bundled about with
their flags, banners, wooden staffs and toy military gear, one
of them intentionally knocked the lead scooter over and it
tipped to the right struck another and led to a domino
affect. Peter's scooter was pinned under the third scooter. He
marched over to the strutting self-important little rooster
that had caused the tumble and spun him around.

"Oi, You shit! Look what you've done!" He screamed
above the blaring propaganda.

Eyes like outraged bullets glared at him. "Shut up!" The
helmeted ultra idiot shouted. They were face to face
screaming at each other.

"If you scratched my scooter, you little jerk, you're
paying to fix it!"

"Piss off!"

"No. Pick up my bike!"

"Piss off, foreigner!" He turned with his group to march
off up the street with their banner.

Peter spun him around and grabbed the side of his
collar and shook the little shit. He threw him around and
the rightist puppet fell over the very scooters he'd knocked
over. "Pick up the goddamn bikes!" A searing whack
wrapped across the back of Peter's thighs and he straightened in pain just as another wooden staff slammed across
the small of his back. He stumbled two steps forward and
reached for the blaring van but it pulled away. Two more
blows thundered down on his side. The scrabbling rat struggled to his feet. He scrambled away trying to make a digni-

fied retreat waving his banner along with two of the other pop-tart militia buffoons that had attacked Peter.

A cavalcade of foul language and guttural yakuza snarl rained on him as they scampered off on their pathetic little protest. Holding his kidneys he bent over and watched as the strutting little cretins receded with their blaring propaganda. He looked around but there was no one paying the least bit of interest to him. Even the sulky girl, who had moments before served him, paid him no heed. The depth of intentionally blind ignorance amazed him. Is it possible to be more blind than just blind? Peter arched back and groaned. There would be a few nasty welts.

A figure rustled beside him and he looked up at the thin bony figure. It was a nondescript, tan, utilitarian type outfit and the wiry man did not glance at Peter as he erected the fallen scooters. In less than a minute, while Peter searched for his bag of cakes, the man re-established the sense of accepted, insanely cluttered, parking mayhem of bikes.

The tan uniform stood before the tall Dane and looked up without any discernible expression in his eyes. They were as devoid of emotion as the noncommittal passersby who had witnessed the whole affair. The bike attendant was about seventy and though withered, he had a distilled sense of decency. "Stupid people." He grumbled in a thick accent. He only had a few words of English. "Crazy people. Very Sorry." The baggy tanned uniform turned and left, gently straightening bikes as he made his way down the street.

Peter started his scooter and glanced back at the Taiyaki shop. He had always thought their cakes were the best, but now he felt annoyed. No, beyond that. They didn't even come out to ask how he was. Were they frightened or just didn't give a damn about others? He pulled away into the midday traffic and charged up Omotesando Avenue in the same direction as the moronic rightists, the Udogokukai as they were known. A vain thought crossed his mind, 'if he passed the van he could kick the side in?' Then again he doubted he could get close enough to withstand the blaring speakers.

THE BRUISING to his back hadn't loosened up at all and though he didn't object to the hard work on the shovel, his mood was less than ebullient. He had no desire to speak to Shimoda, his colleague, sweating at the handle of the other shovel. Shimoda was a fit man of about forty-five and could shovel like a demon. Peter spent most of his time staring at the bald scalp wrapped in a band of white terry-towel. The man never took a break; he was a virtual mechanical digger. To Peter, Shimoda was as obsessed with the shovel as the rightists were with their damn speakers.

"That should be enough, just clean up the edges and we can line it tomorrow." It was Thys Rasmussen. Peter had not even heard him approach. Thys, now in his late seventies had just returned from the far end of the garden where he had spent the last two hours maintaining his beloved bonsai. Peter knew little of the technique, but had always been fascinated by the intense character cultivated in each tree. Even his co-worker, the mad digger Shimoda, revered the skills of the old man with a near godlike capacity.

"Thys are you sure this pool is going to be for carp and not sharks or even whales?"

"Maybe he wants to go sailing," Shimoda added. Peter found it amusing and they both laughed with the old man.

"Carp need space to grow," Thys countered. "You can't treat carp like bonsai."

"Pity, it would be easier on our backs," said Peter. Shimoda laughed and slapped Peter casually on the back. "Eeaah!" Peter screamed.

"What? You can't be that stiff. You're young," Shimoda said.

"Nah, I had a bit of trouble this morning, see." Peter lifted his shirt and showed the welts on his back. "Check this out. Hurts like hell."

"Christ!" Thys exclaimed as he turned Peter around for Shimoda to see his back.

"Waa! That's bad. Did you fall off your scooter?"

"Peter, what've you done to yourself?" Thys' wife Chieko, had seen his back from the tearoom where she was preparing their end of day treat.

"Ah, bit of trouble with some ultra rightists." There was an odd stillness among them. It descended abruptly. Peter didn't understand it, but it was one of those vacuous moments in a conversation where everyone suddenly chooses not to participate and a chasm swallows everyone.

Shimoda crossed away with the tools. "You must be careful in mixing with things you don't understand."

"Where's the understanding here? That's an attack." Thys glared directly at Shimoda, who was intent on slithering away.

"I don't know anything about it." Shimoda wandered off with the two shovels.

"Come up here Peter, I'll put some cream on it." Chieko Rasmussen called from the open veranda leading off the tearoom.

"It's okay, I'll be fine."

"Get up there and take your shirt off or she'll give you another beating." Thys warned him. Thys raised his voice slightly and turned to the slim figure poised in a lime green summer kimono. "If you're going to last around here, Peter, you'll have to learn who is the enforcer of the house. Isn't that right Chieko, darling?" His humor was met with a cold taut glare. Thys didn't mind, he just sniggered knowingly to the lanky younger man. Peter had immediately twigged to the fact that they had a very close and intense relationship for an older couple. Thys waved Peter up and onto the veranda. "Please."

MRS. RASMUSSEN WAS EXTREMELY gentle in the application of the cream and he only winced a few times. Oddly, he wanted to appear strong in front of the older woman. Though she was in her seventies, she was a remarkably handsome woman and was the embodiment of everything Peter perceived as beautiful in Japan. Everything except one — she had opinions that fired out of her like a shotgun. Thys was the gentle affable scientist, with a deep well of knowledge and understanding about his field of marine biology, as well as a staggering knowledge of the Orient. Having immersed himself for over forty years in the culture of Japan. He was more Japanese than the Japanese. Certainly his capabilities in gardening and literature left him revered over any other Japanophile. Peter also knew of Thys' history with the royal family and the close friendship and scientific studies he'd conducted with Emperor Hirohito. His wife, Chieko, was from an aristocratic samurai family, the Ashikagas, at one time a powerful shogunate, and she was immensely respected wherever she traveled. Though Peter had only been in Japan a month and only out in public with her and Thys twice, it proved to be an enlightening and somewhat intimidating experience. Thys was treated with the venerated, monk-like respect one would afford a master of arts, but his wife was approached like a caged tiger. She was viewed as a being of mystery, respect and in some aspects, outright fear. Peter quickly gathered that great women of culture and birthright could still carry that gravitas in Japan.

Chieko applied the cream over the wide, muscled, young torso. She admonished him for his naivety. "The rightists are buffoons. Why did you let yourself get caught up in it?"

"He tipped over an entire row of scooters, mine was in the middle of it."

"No one came to help you?" Thys asked.

"No. Well, it happened so fast and I was smacked from behind."

"You should have stayed out of it," Chieko repeated tersely.

"I didn't try to get into it, believe me."

"No one helped you?" Thys asked again as if by repeating it he could change the answer.

"Those groups are nuts and should be banned," Peter mumbled.

"The pathetic worms that watched should also be punished. Why do we have to put up with such cowards? Both sides are disgusting boneless vermin." Chieko's opinions thundered.

"Yes, dear."

"Don't talk to me like that Thys." She continued unconcerned about Peter's presence. "You allow Shimoda to work here and he is as backward as the rest of them."

"But he's a good gardener. He has an understanding with plants." Thys' demeanor swelled with a sense of rotund Buddhist understanding. He looked at his wife as if peering from the surface of a still pond. He waited for her anticipated response.

"He's an idiot and supports them. He should be sacked, weeded out."

"Shimodasan is an ultra rightist?" Peter blurted out.

"He was involved with them years ago, but not anymore."

She cut him off. "They're like a cancer, once in your system they can't be eradicated."

With the subtlest of openings of his palm he calmed the tiger. "Chieko, how about we put this down to a crude lesson and enjoy the taiyaki treat that Peter brought?"

Peter could feel the cold breeze of her emotionless stare drift over his shoulder toward Thys, who knelt in front of him across the low table. It was an icy chill that failed to ripple the surface of the old man's temperament. A cement curtain had lowered on the conversation. Thys' smile was a blend of condescension and compassion. Chieko's voice floated like a wind chime to match her husband's smile. "We are fortunate to have such a thoughtful assistant, even if he has a colorful back." Chieko then stood and left the room to get the Taiyaki. A truce had been brokered.

The paper shoji slid closed and Peter leaned forward to rest his arms on the low table. "What's it all about Thys? I've studied for six years and I can't understand the blaring crap they spew from those speakers."

The gentle older man drew a slow breath to distill his thoughts. He had adopted the Japanese custom of audibly drawing a breath when ruminating on a thought. Peter remembered it was 'haragei' a kind of stomach communication. It was the way trust was established by parties in conversation. Good 'haragei' superseded honorable handshakes and chivalry. Peter had read that, though the West believes access to the soul is through the eyes, the East believes the real communication happens at man's gravitational center, the stomach. Thys had lived in Japan long enough to relish the imparting of wisdom. "It is actually quite simple, they have issues that relate primarily to the role of the Emperor. They want him reinstated as an all-powerful god-like individual. He is the embodiment of the Japanese way, the bushido spirit." The white paper shoji slid open and he stopped immediately. A splinter of warning flashed through his eyes to Peter. Chieko entered.

Chieko knelt by the table and presented some fruit and Taiyaki on two square platters. The exquisite design of the platters made the Taiyaki look woeful. "I recognized the store where you picked up these treats. We've not been there for years. Thys insists on the shop in Ueno Park, but this shop is also very well known. Perhaps your stomach is more Japanese than you realize. That is a good thing. They are a wonderful treat. We mustn't let Thys get fat though, he did no shoveling today."

"Enough Chieko, don't you have a calligraphy exhibit to attend?" He prodded.

"Ah, the guilt in his voice is thick. Yes dear, I do." Her look carried the same condescension his had. They were an ideal couple. She nodded slightly to her husband and then turned to Peter. "I will apply more cream to your back tomorrow."

"I'll be fine, really."

"I will apply more cream to your back tomorrow." There was a muffled snigger from Thys. She flashed a glare at him. "After you have helped Thys tomorrow, would you like to attend a Kendo match with me? Thys has a meeting and one of my students is competing."

"Students?" The old man chucked softly. Peter wasn't sure why, but the old man was enjoying the provocative banter of his lovely wife.

"Yes, Thys. A student." Peter sensed an odd glimmer between them. He had learned in the brief month with them, as their gardening assistant, that even in their senior years they sparked a fiery passion off each other. Peter thought it would be wise to not get caught between them – ever. "It will only be for an hour and will be most entertaining."

"I'd love to. I've never seen kendo."

"You'll love it, Peter. It's very forceful and direct. Chieko was very accomplished as a young woman."

"Was?" Chieko paused to allow him to grin back at her.

"Excuse me." He stuttered barely able to hold his grin.

She rose in one fluid movement as only women trained in Oriental etiquette can. She bowed and left the room. Peter thought he detected the hint of a loving grin from her toward the old man.

"As I was saying. The ultra rightists want to move Japan back a hundred years."

"But I thought MacArthur had stamped out all vestiges of Imperial Japan."

"Well, judging from your back, he failed. But in truth he just drove them off into different corners to hide. You can't destroy a thousand years of history with a few decrees, hastily thrown together by people with no understanding of the country. Simply toss together a constitution and apply it. They did it in a week, you know. Twenty-four men and women, only one of whom spoke or understood the Japanese. She was twenty-two years old and educated in an international school. Is that honoring the tradition of two thousand years? The inept Japanese government just rubber stamped it."

"But I thought the Japanese people wanted the new constitution? I read that they virtually worshipped

MacArthur and SCAP, the whole occupational forces effort."

"True to a degree. It was a strange time to be in Japan. I wish I could've also been here in the late eighteen hundreds, a similar time of turmoil. Looking back at the early fifties I was amazed that the Japanese politicians were so hopeless, so castrated, so impotent." He shook his head, he had been more vitriolic than he had intended. "Well, they have always been spineless, all politicians in truth are, regardless of nationality. Self preservation and advancement seem to eclipse morality in Japanese politicians."

"I don't doubt that. But what about the Emperor? What were his opinions of these nutcases in their vans tearing around the streets? I don't want to pry, I know he was a close friend."

"Yes, he was a close friend. I don't want to talk about him now. He was a great friend and we shared many hours together. We should never talk about him in the same breath as these ultra rightist idiots."

"But I thought –"

"Not today Peter and never in front of Chieko, that is, if you value your life." He laughed to himself and shook his head. "She is a direct descendant of the Ashikaga shoguns. Sometimes I think she hasn't left that period."

"She is an amazing woman."

"Amazingly what? Brutal? Frightening?"

"No – well, a bit. But Beautiful."

"Oh yes. The Ashikaga women were known for their beauty, even in the fourteenth century. But they also had some attitude problems. They have a bit of a chip on their shoulder from their first shogun, Ashikaga Takauji. He was known as a treacherous traitor, a villain. As recent as a hundred years ago they were decapitating his statues in

Japan. But regardless of that, they were a very noble family. You should research it and then never, ever, mention it in her presence."

"Sounds dangerous."

"Not at all, but it does show how slowly things die in this country. It's the same in Europe. Especially eastern Europe, the hatreds there die very slow deaths."

"All I wanted was Taiyaki."

"Well you came to Japan with a great understanding of the language. Now you must get to know the people and their history, and maybe how confused they are about it themselves."

2

P eter left his scooter in the parking bay in front of his apartment and walked around the brick balustrade. The scooter was his best purchase upon arrival in Tokyo. He picked it up in a 'sayonara sale' in the Daily Yomiuri, one of the lifeline newspapers for the expat community, along with a telephone line connection and fax. In fact he had been able to set himself up on a shoestring, though the size of his apartment wasn't much more than a shoebox itself. He was a bachelor and student, so he could survive in it. It was less for him to clean and that was a definite bonus.

He pushed his key into the heavy brown metal door. Another scooter roared into the little parking area shared by the eight occupants of the little block. The landlord had a really good scam going Peter thought. With each apartment being a 1DK as they called it, which was actually a small studio, he had jammed eight over-priced rental units into an area the size of two large garages. Even compared to Copenhagen, the apartments were hopelessly small. In Copenhagen you could find lower-end places of about thirty-five square meters. This place would struggle to make twenty.

The scooter driver was his neighbor from two doors down, Sammy. He came around the corner with his helmet still on. "Hey, Peter."

"Hi ya, Sammy." They spoke in Japanese, as his English was hopeless and like so many Indians every verb was in the progressive, so one could never really tell the time of any particular conversation.

"You want to go to the Sento?" They had been to the public bath three or four times already. It was a good way to chill out at the end of the day.

"Ah no, not tonight. I got a little roughed up today."

"Oh yeah, a Roppongi girl? I told you to stay away from them."

"Very funny. No some ultra rightists."

"That was stupid. I'd prefer the Roppongi girl."

"Yeah, me too. Maybe we could have a beer later? I need to chill out."

"Sure. I've got to study anyway. We'll watch the sumo at ten twenty."

"Great. Later."

PETER WENT into his little studio and was greeted by a welcoming futon that had been very carefully left in exactly the same position as the night before, in fact the week before. It took no time at all to collapse onto it and go to sleep; face down. The shoveling and the whacking put him into a deep consuming splendor of oblivion.

Two brief hours later the familiar clack, clack, clack of the cedar batons pulled him from his sleep. The open windows and paper-thin walls allowed an immediacy and intimacy with one's neighbors that Peter was still adjusting to. The clacking was from the opening ceremony of 'Sumo

Digest' and the girls who shared the place next door were watching it on TV. They were already giggling and obviously having a beer. It would be a single beer he thought. The Japanese he had met were not particularly good at holding alcohol and would glow red in no time, though not necessarily be drunk. He thought about Sammy, grabbed a large bottle of Kirin lager beer from his fridge and went around to his studio flat to interrupt his studies.

Sammy loved watching the Sumo wrap up at the end of the day. He often went to watch live matches when the Basho came to Tokyo. He had promised to take Peter to the tournament one day. The two-week summer Basho was in Tokyo now, hopefully they could drop around and get some cheap nose-bleeder seats at the top. Peter had heard the prices were outrageous.

Sammy had settled down in front of the television having forsaken his books for the Sumo report. Peter waved the bottle and Sammy ushered him across the tiny kitchen to the floor in front of the TV. They cracked the beer and Sammy explained the background of some of the wrestlers. After losing one hundred yen at ten yen bets, Peter wondered if Sammy had already seen the results somewhere. The beer was good and the dried squid and sembe crackers went down as a suitable substitute for a proper meal. After a few more drinks to drain the massive one liter bottle they parted, and Peter wandered down the short walkway to his apartment. The door in front of him opened suddenly and the two girls, clad in summer yukata, a kind of light kimono, stepped out. It startled all three of them. They were obviously going to the public bath and had a washbasin in their arms filled with toiletries and small towels. He liked the two girls. He didn't find either of them attractive, but they were still girls and it was easy for him to be polite.

He consciously focused on their faces and not the their bodies, which pushed out through the thin fabric. They were young, only just twenty, and too giggly for him. Perhaps it was because he was a foreigner that they acted so immature. In any event, once they turned to leave, he found himself watching their bodies as they slipped down the hallway made by the overhanging second floor. They were young women, but then a woman of any age was something he had not had for far too long. Immersing himself in his masters had limited his social life prior to the chance of coming to study at Sophia University in Tokyo.

Back in his room the beer and shoveling of the day raced forward and stamped his mind into a dull submission as he fell asleep. He should study some Kanji, but Japanese calligraphy did not hold the spark needed to turn on the light, not tonight anyway.

3

Mrs. Rasmussen insisted on Peter taking a shower before they left for the kendo tournament. In her polite, direct manner she stated that, 'he smelled like a man who had been working all day and she preferred the smell of a man who had been thinking all day.' Then she passed him a towel and directed him to the bathroom. Peter didn't put up a fight, the day had been one long hard slog.

After his morning class at Sophia University he had scootered across to the Rasmussen's to help Thys with the lining of the pool. It had been a torturous four hours, with Shimoda giving all the orders of how the pool was to be constructed and Peter doing all the spadework. Shimoda got some kind of thrill out of barking out orders and on more than one occasion, he reminded Peter of the strutting little martinets who had attacked him from behind. Once the lining was in and the two pumps in place it was just a matter of cleaning up, but Shimoda had somehow disappeared and Peter was left to finish it off himself. It had taken longer than he thought and when Chieko found he was still working, she insisted he hurry and take a shower. She would not accept being made late by a carp pool.

***

THE GLASS DOORS at the entrance to the Kendo hall were obviously new and swooshed smoothly allowing a rush of cool air to wash over them as he ushered Chieko through. The genkan or entrance area, was broad and lined on both sides with hundreds of customary locked shoeboxes. There was not a wayward shoe or sandal in the entire entrance. Discipline was painfully apparent.

Chieko was known at the center and the moment they entered, two young girls, still wearing their kendo armor, scurried over to greet them. The girls bowed deeply to Chieko and offered slippers for them both. The young girls, no more than fourteen, giggled quietly at the sight of the spindly blond foreigner. They were led down the corridor to the main hall and ushered to two square zabuton cushions. Chieko in her grace slithered effortlessly down and sat seiza in a most elegant of manner. Peter struggled with the whole kneeling issue and though he tried, a pathetic smirk from Chieko allowed him to sit cross-legged. A cool face cloth was brought on a tray and a cup of chilled tea with a sweet was laid beside them. The serving students scurried away and Chieko settled to watch the training session. Peter noticed a handful of others seated in various areas of the hall all intently watching the students who were practicing in groups.

At first Peter thought it was all a bit of show, with lots of

high-pitched screaming and smacking of bamboo swords.
To him it didn't seem to be a dangerous martial art as such.
It was all a bit of pageantry. There was a tap on the side of
his knee and Chieko pointed to two Kendoka who were
centering themselves for a bout in the middle of the room.
All the other bouts soon fell into silence and muffled
rumble of feet ensued as all the students formed a large
circle around the two swordsman in the center. The students
all sat on cue. Peter assumed these were two of the more
advanced swordsman as an air of reverence calmly perme-
ated the hall. Both Kendoka swordsmen were draped
entirely in heavy blue fabric and had shiny chest plates,
with armored shoulder padding and long protective gloves.
Their faces were shrouded in a Darth Vader-type wire mesh
mask. They looked like Jedi nights with long bamboo
swords. Peter wondered if he was missing something as
Thys had said it would be impressive, it was all a bit tame.
The hall fell to total silence and Peter thought that obviously the master was to give an instruction to the assembled
group.

After their bows there was a long stillness. Neither
fighter moved an inch. Peter wondered if they had forgot to
do something, like fight? He was just losing interest and
shifted his weight on the cushion when an almighty scream
erupted from one of the blue draped figures and a whirl of
blows rained across the mat driving the other Kendoka
backward. Then stillness resumed. Peter hadn't taken a
breath. An explosion erupted again from the same Kendoka
but this time the other fighter responded in attack and a
lightning trade of blows and parries shattered around the
room. The Hall came alive with screams and the continual
reverberation of bamboo on bamboo. It was like machine
gun fire. Peter was staggered by the volcanic eruption of

excitement and fear within him. Both swordsmen were like bottled dynamite or nitroglycerin, whatever it was, when the cap came off, it was violent. He worried about whether the armor would be strong enough to withstand the power of the blows. It was terrifying to watch the intent and aggression of the Kendoka swordsmen. He glanced at Chieko who stared impassively at the fight without flinching at the cracking that echoed off the walls. '*They were trying to bash the hell out of each other*' Peter thought. The younger livelier Kendoka was on the back foot and was losing position and composure to the calmer shorter Kendoka. In what looked like a zealous attempt to win back control the younger Kendoka appeared too aggressive and made for an attack. In a flash the attacker was skewered by the short Kendoka with a thrust to the throat. The shorter calmer Kendoka held the younger, more vibrant Kendoka in the position of humiliation for a few moments before gracefully retracting. The match was over and Peter was literally in a seizure of excitement. He relaxed and looked at Chieko who watched calmly. She turned to face him, a swan gazing gracefully at the flustered frog beside her. She smiled at Peter.

"Good match, wasn't it?"

"Fantastic. Are they okay? They could have killed one another, especially with the thrust to the throat."

"No, they are fine. She is fine, just her pride is hurt. She is out of practice, she's been away too long. Nevertheless she will sulk. So she should too."

"She?" Peter couldn't possibly imagine that one of the growling, barking swordsman was female. Chieko saw his confusion and nodded to the center. The wire grilled mask and headpiece was removed and both fighters were bowing to one another. They faced away and the short buzzed grey hair of the winning Kendoka, obviously the master, was giving instruction to the other. It was the other Kendoka that amazed him. An enormous wave of hair trailed down her back and he realized for the first time it was a woman. As if she sensed his stare, she bowed to the master and walked briskly across to Chieko and Peter. The master stepped to one side and bowed to Chieko who returned his bow with her typical slow held grace. Peter stared like an idiot but couldn't shake the sense of wonder. What a being! His mind jammed.

"Thank you for coming. I apologize for my perfor-mance." The mane of hair flooded forward as the defeated Kendoka bowed humbly.

Peter was floating at the sight of her.

"No, no." Chieko took the young girl's chin and raised it to smile at her. "I didn't think you should've gone straight into it after returning. I am sure sensei told you off."

"Yes, I have to do extra training. He says I've gotten worse since I've been training in the States. I am not on center."

"Of course, that was clear. But it was still very good. The power of your kiai scream is shattering; just not quite on center." Chieko realized Peter was standing beside them, towering over them both. "Oh, Sorry. This is Peter, the assistant I was telling you about from Denmark."

The young woman turned her eyes directly up at Peter and he felt he had lost his way. The eyes bombarded his mind with thoughts, wonder and images. "Hi Peter, I've heard all about you."

'She knew about him. How glorious' he thought. He looked at her, he wasn't sure what else to do.

"Hello?" She repeated as she tried to break his stare.

"Hi, I mean, hello. I've never met anyone so violent. I mean so beautifully violent, in a good sense. The beautiful and the violent." Peter wondered if he sounded like an idiot.

"Peter now would be a good time to shake her hand and just shut up," Chieko said.

Peter put out his hand and the powerful young girl grabbed it. His hand went numb with a flush of confused emotions. Chieko turned the young woman away and walked her across to the sensei. Chieko stopped and turned back to the vacant minded young Dane. "Peter, my grand-daughter Rie will join me for a snack on the way home, can you join us?" Peter nodded too eagerly. "Work on your artic-ulation until we get back."

"See you later Peter, thanks for coming," Rie remarked innocently, completely aware what she had done to Peter's 'center'. It was totally knocked askew. He could only smile at her. He watched them walk across the hall and went over in his mind what he knew. She was Rie, granddaughter, killer Kendoka and dream of a woman. At that point his mind jammed shut.

***

CHIEKO TOOK them to a small teahouse in Shitamachi, the old quarter of Tokyo. The shop only had four tables inside and an equal number of cement benches arranged in the inner courtyard. The proprietors fussed over Rie and her return from America. They were obviously regulars at the shop and moved straight through to the courtyard. Two of the other cement benches had guests. Peter's heart, racing from the proximity of Rie, was stilled as soon as he stepped into the courtyard. Tranquility seeped into the moss. The rocks were polished and yet retained brooding features, a supported pine bough was suspended across the back wall on short stilts. A single wind chime sang a song of lazy summer heat. The subtle whisper from the chime welcomed the season and imbued the garden with an all-encompassing serenity interrupted by the trickle from the takenoko fountain. The takenoko was a simple bamboo shaft anchored at a forty-degree angle with water trickling in to it. Once filled it would tip forward, empty and clunk back to refill. It was the sound of the clunk, when it landed that Peter found spellbinding. It clunked three times. Loudly and then two light short follow-up raps. The sound was the voice of the garden. The enchanting sound controlled the pulse of everything in the garden – except his thoughts of Rie.

They had shaved ice, Kakigori, and though he was included in the conversation most of it drifted by. He wasn't sure if he was mesmerized by the effect of Rie or if it was the grace of Chieko or the embalming tranquility of the surroundings. In any event his thoughts were swimming. He focused on the dessert. The shaved ice cream was splendid. He'd had Kakigori a few times, but didn't think it held a spot against Ben and Jerry's or Hagen Das, but this was different. The azuki sweet beans and condensed milk swirled against the cold green tea flavored ice crystals to make a precocious taste explosion.

"He has no idea."

Peter looked at the two women realizing they were actually talking about him. "What?"

Rie pointed her spoon at his dessert, "You may know your Taiyaki, but you know nothing about Kakigori."

"It's fantastic."

"It's how you eat it. I thought you Danes knew about desserts. You know 'the land of pastries' and all that." Rie was winding him up. "Here." She leaned close and dug a small tunnel in the ice of his dish. Peter was dizzied by the fragrance of her hair, it wasn't artificial, it refreshed him like the lushness of a fresh cut lawn. Her proximity made him thankful they were sitting down. Rie knew he was rippling with an innocent flush. "You have to dig down under and get to the azuki beans, let it mix with the milk and then drag it up through the green tea and then eat it." She raised the spoon to his lips. He stared at her like an idiot. "Open your mouth stupid." She slipped the spoon between his lips. "That, is how you eat Kakigori."

"You're such a tease Rie. I hope that is not all you've learned in New York."

"Gran! No of course not. Besides their shaved ice is crap."

"Let me try." Peter, realizing he was being mocked by the young enchantress, dug his spoon into the bottom of her dessert and scooped a huge spoonful of the prized azuki paste, drug it through the milk and woofed the enormous load down in one cavernous gulp. Chieko howled.

"What're you doing? You jerk?" Rie barked in English. Peter couldn't speak his mouth was full and frozen. He muffled a protest. "You took all my Azuki! You shit!" Rie was fuming. She glanced at her grandmother then back at the grinning Peter. "You swine." Peter laughed. Chieko could hardly stay in her seat. Rie's anger erupted simultaneously in English and Japanese. She slapped Peter's back, directly on the welts from yesterday. He screamed and jumped out of his seat. "It wasn't that hard you wimp! A thief and a wimp. Where'd you find him Gran?" She returned protectively to her dessert.

Peter was still trying to control his frozen mouth while gently rubbing his back.

"He got a bad beating yesterday. Seems he mixed it up with some ultra rightists. They whacked his back, just where you did."

"God! A wimp, thief and an idiot!" She softened her glare. "Sorry about the slap Peter, but you did steal my Azuki, so you're not off the hook." She reached over and scooped his. He was still in shock and couldn't protest.

The remainder of the dessert was spent discussing New York and the garden, and not a mention was made of the kendo match. Peter, though he was included in the conversation, spent most of the time listening to the laughter of the two women that bubbled forth like clouds drifting on a summer sky. Peter felt for the first time in his life, he was smitten with a woman. He bathed in the feeling of being completely enthralled by Rie. He noticed how she was so much like her grandmother – a combination of beauty and violence, pride and subtlety, serenity and arrogance. Peter thought he must not be seen as swept off his feet. So he chose to remain aloof and focused on the garden and away from her ebony eyes. Chieko slipped away to pay the proprietor and left the youngsters for a few moments.

Peter watched the serene Chieko retreat into the shop and seized his opportunity. "Can I make up for the theft and take you for coffee later? That's if you have no other plans. I'm sure you're tired or jet lagged, so if you don't want to—"

Rie put her hand up to stop him. "I'll make my own excuses thanks Peter. Women are good at that."

He deflated. "Well? Do you want to meet at nine at Hachiko Square?"

"Sure, nine is fine. I guess I'll have to get along with you, as I'll be staying with grandma all summer."

"I'll try to make it easy for you and only steal your Azuki on Wednesdays and Fridays."

"Hah! You've had the only bit you'll ever get."

They both laughed. Peter thought her smile and genuineness was truly gorgeous. Everything about her was.

***

HACHIKO SQUARE IS the central meeting destination in Shibuya and the place heaves with bodies from morning until morning. It was the only place Peter knew off the top of his head. The central statue, 'Hachiko' was erected for a small dog honored by the local police. Hachiko's master was accompanied faithfully by the little dog to the station each and everyday. There the dog waited until his return from work and they trotted home together. The friendship lasted for years, until one day it all stopped. The master had gone to work as usual in a factory, during the war. He bid goodbye to Hachiko at the station and never returned. The police watched the faithful dog wait for his master everyday until the dog could survive no longer. Hachiko pined for her master, constantly watching and waiting, immoveable, until at last the little dog died. The police stationed in the nearby police box were devastated to see the faithful little dog's loyalty finally defeated by death. They raised the funds for her statue and it was now, at Hachiko's feet, that Peter leaned, while he waited for Rie.

Peter wasn't the type to swoon blindly for a girl, in fact, he had never really chased a girl. The idea of having your brain and heart turned on its head in confusion in a few seconds was not for him. He still thought he could play the field. But, then, Rie was different, she was altogether different.

"Hi ya."

He turned, it was Rie. She was dressed more casually and he tried to look calm but his eyes betrayed him. He wasn't so base as to give her an up and down look – he'd done that in the ice sweet shop. His eyes betrayed him because they wanted to rivet or glue to hers and he felt being entranced made him appear stupid. He wouldn't have blamed her if she tried to slap him awake. "Do you want to go to Starbucks?"

"God, no." Rie said frankly. Peter was taken aback and hadn't really got another suggestion. Starbucks were everywhere in Tokyo, like a disease. There was only one in Denmark and that was at the airport. Still their frappacinos were great and on a student budget they were reasonable. Rie saw his shock. "I can go to a Starbucks anywhere. Gran says you have a scooter?" He nodded and she wrapped her arm in his. "Good you drive, I'll give directions. My friend has a small funky 'kissaten'-type coffee shop in Ebisu about ten minutes from here. You'll love it."

He started the scooter and felt her arm wrap tentatively around his waist for support. There was a flush of heat behind his eyes. It was quickly shattered though by the thrust of her other arm. It shot out in front of his face.

"That way Tonto!" She giggled.

Rie knew her destinations. It was a great choice and not one that he made very often as he opted for the trendy western chains. 'Kissaten' in Japan are old-fashioned private coffee houses, where individual service and the idea of spending time over a coffee is as important as the individually roasted blends. Coffee at a Kissaten was usually triple the price, but came with an array of complimentary dishes

or 'services', which invariably kept you there for two hours.
The interior of Rie's friend's place was done in a decadent,
shabby-chic, French grunge. All the chairs were rococo
refits, covered in luscious colors and bold stripes or fake fur.
It was the kind of place Andy Warhol's grandmother might
own. One thing he had discovered in his month here, was
that the Japanese loved their hybrid designs and they were
fantastic at creating them. The trend of all too similar Scandinavian lines was nowhere in Tokyo.

It was when her friend came to warn them about the last
train times, that they realized they had been chatting for
three hours. Time, like water striking scorching pavement,
had just vanished. They paid and walked out into the
stifling summer night. She jumped on the scooter, eager to
get out and on the streets. She was obviously quite taken by
the bike. She was a tantalizing sight he thought. He weaved
the scooter through the glaring neon Tokyo streets. He
gazed forward at the street and focused backward on his
passenger. A gang of six Bosozoku bikes, with their cut
mufflers howling, rapped a vicious snarl beside them as they
lined up at one of the lights. Peter just smiled blandly
ignoring their intimidating quaffed hair and leathers. As the
gang tore off she tightened her arms around his waist and
leaned into his back.

"Those guys are a joke," she yelled over the engine.

"Yeah, baby mafia, they'd get their asses kicked in any
other country." They roared along under the expressway.
Scattered under the cement columns of the overhead
highway was a row of Yatai stands and he thought she might
be hungry. The little Yatai carts, set up all over the city to do
a bit of evening trade, usually catered to drunken, exhausted
businessmen struggling home. The Yatai cart's water
supplies were limited and hygiene questionable, but the

temporary wooden roofs with beer crate stools, smoking cookers and lonely night lanterns were as much a figure of Japanese lifestyle as cherry blossoms – though nowhere near as stately. These rickety carts were the basest connection, for the exhausted office termite, to a simpler land of country cooking. He slowed and twisted back to face her. She was very close. "Do you want some oden or soba?"

She shook her head. "Na, I'm tired I just want to go home."

"Cool." He pulled away swiftly and her grip tightened. His mind was consumed by the softness of her arms around his waist. Those same arms that thundered blows on the poor little man on the kendo floor before he thrust a sword at her jugular and yet her arms pulsed a warmth through him. When he stopped in front of the house, she quickly slipped off and only then did he feel the coolness on the outside of his thighs where her legs had been pressed. He felt aroused by the thought of her holding him. She stood in front of the scooter, the headlight flared up to her as she took her helmet off. Her hair flowed around her and swayed across her neck in the light evening breeze. Her face appeared to float on the light. She touched his arm in a sisterly fashion.

"Thanks for tonight, it was fun."

"Yeah, thanks Rie," he paused unsure of his chances with such a creature. "Maybe we could—"

She held up a finger and pointed sternly at him. "You still owe me." She crossed to the entrance of Thys' stately old house. "Tonight wasn't even half a spoonful of Azuki." She smiled and slid the exterior door open.

Peter smiled back, hit the scooter start button and drove home.

She consumed his thoughts. In some way she had

ravaged his mind. He rolled his eyes, even he thought he was being pathetic. Though he knew the route well, by the time he slowed in front of his apartment block he realized he didn't remember any of the journey. He made the turns and saw the buildings, but his mind was in a trance. He was intoxicated by a dizzy array of her bubbling laughter, her smile, her eyes, the endless gorgeous flowing hair that fell across her shoulders and the smooth grace of her neck. If Modigliani ever came to Japan he would have been captivated. He parked his scooter and wandered, almost love drunk, to his futon, neatly positioned from last night. Peter collapsed onto it and a world of possibilities welcomed him to a dreamy sleep, face down.

4

Morning arrived with a scream from his body. The heavy shoveling and the beating all combined to give him the feeling he had slept in a lobster crate. Every fiber of muscle in his body voiced its protest against movement of any sort. He stumbled to the unit bathroom and sneered at the poor excuse for a shower. In Denmark the concept of an open wet-room was a delight for mornings such as this. All one had to do was stagger straight in, turn the tap and stand. It was quite simply a kind of early morning glory. These prefabricated unit baths were tiny, deep and inevitably the nozzle sprayed as much on the floor as it did on the body. It was like standing in a bucket and showering. Climbing over the side into the tub brought a chorus of complaint from his muscles. Hot water was what he needed to persuade his body to shut up and let him get to classes and then over to Thys' to work, so he could then see Rie.

***

FOR SOME UNKNOWN reason Shimoda had not appeared for work, so it was just Peter and Thys working in the garden. It was fortunate for Peter as it allowed him time to find out more about Rie from the old man.

The mood in the rear garden among the bonsai was more restrained and reflective. Hovering around Thys, Peter did what he could. The old man pottered in a considered thoughtful conversation with each plant

"Can you hold this wire, Peter?"

Peter crossed to him and held one end of the wire while the other was carefully manipulated and curled around the base of the bonsai trunk. Being no more than thirty centimeters high it was a delicate process to position the tiny T' shaped post to support the extending finger-like branch of the bonsai. The gnarled branch grew at a right angle to the base and was twenty centimeters in length. It was a stunning feature of the stately dwarf pine. The small branch, in its simplicity, was able to visually balance the much larger trunk. Though he struggled with the technical aspects of bonsai, he had already, through his time with Thys, gained an appreciation of the intricate harmony and asymmetrical balances required to produce a unique bonsai.

"So what do you think of her?" Thys asked as he turned the bonsai, admiring his work.

"You must be very proud." Thys nodded to himself and examined the sprinkle of emerald moss on the rocky outcropping surrounding the base. With a small skewer he gently pushed on a filament of moss. Peter continued, "stunning, really. If I may say so."

"Well, we all need to learn how to appreciate beauty."

"Yes," Peter was not looking at the bonsai, his gaze had drifted up the garden toward the new carp pool construction and the veranda of the old ash colored house. "There's an air of playful sophistication."

Thys cocked his head up from the bonsai toward Peter. "Playful?"

"Mmm. It's as if there was danger and beauty rolled into one."

Thys could see that Peter was not even looking at the dwarf pine and was in an altogether different space. "The bonsai? I'm talking about the bonsai, not Rie."

The sound of her name made Peter snap around. He realized he'd made a fool of himself. "Eh?" Embarrassment struggled with his dream and he floundered for cover. "Yes, of course, me too; the bonsai."

"Oh, good," Thys played with Peter's embarrassment. "So what do you think of Rie or have you any opinions after your first few meetings?"

"She's a very... " he was desperate to not say the same thing, but couldn't trust his mouth, "nice girl, fantastic actually. She's very easy to get along with."

"Ha! She's a nightmare like her mother and grandmother."

"Well, she's a little headstrong."

"Little headstrong? You mean stubborn or belligerent."

"No, I never said that."

"Nor would you, or I for that matter, if we did, all three of them would come and get us. Probably skewer us with their damn kendo swords!" Both men laughed softly. Peter felt a touch awkward in front of Thys, he was still her grandfather. Peter returned to cleaning around the bonsai bases. After the mention of Rie they both fell silent and each resumed their separate jobs. Trimming the bonsai roots and repotting them was a slow and meditative practice.

Peter found it easy to lose himself in the simplicity of design and the intense majesty of the miniature trees. Each time he looked at the twisted wizened tree trunks, he felt a warmth well inside him to have her arms around him again, as on the scooter last night. It was just a scooter ride, but it was more than that too.

"You are working slowly today, Peter. Something on your mind?"

"Ah, no, no. Just thinking."

"A dangerous practice. Could you go and ask Rie to bring some tea down to us?"

"OF COURSE." Peter's melancholy drift evaporated instantly with the prospect of going to the house and seeing Rie. He dashed from the secluded corner of the garden where the bonsai rows were located. As he approached the house he saw Rie sitting seiza in the day room across the veranda. The room was sparse and she was centered in the room, surrounded by the tawny yellow tetami mats. She wore a plain blue yukatta with tiny pink butterflies. For a modern woman she was uniquely old fashioned, he thought. She was focusing over a table with a long fude brush in her hand, obviously practicing her calligraphy. Calligraphy or shuji in Japanese was an art not only of the grace and structure of the characters, but also of what is said and how it is said in a few strokes. Peter had struggled with the concept, but like bonsai, though he understood it, developing an appreciation and capability, was a life long challenge for a practitioner. There were numerous papers scattered nearby, only two hanging to dry.

She was obviously not happy with her work. Her demeanor appeared very calm and serene, yet she was troubled and moved another paper to one side. Frustration or preoccupation were filtering into her shuji work. She took a deep breath and peered over the garden. It was then that she saw him staring at her.

"Good morning, Peter."

"Hi. You looked very lost in your work, I didn't want to disturb."

"Then why did you?"

He detected a bite in her voice that was not there when they parted the night before. "I didn't, I was watching you. You stopped. Obviously troubled by something, perhaps your work."

"Do you understand shuji, calligraphy?"

"I don't understand anything, I'm learning." He thought this would be the safest track with her volatile personality.

"Well, in any case my work this morning is crap. I'm not focusing or focusing so much I'm... unfocused."

"Maybe it has to do with your loss in Kendo."

She glared at him and stood up. She crossed slowly to the edge of the low veranda and looked down at him. He saw the fine white tabi socks on her feet. To him they looked dainty, but knowing what little he did of her, he wasn't sure there was anything 'dainty' about this woman. It was only yesterday he had seen her stomping and slashing. When he looked back up at her face, the alluring eyes he had hoped to see were spitting poison at him. It was like the cobras he had seen on the Discovery channel that blind their prey.

"So, are you now an expert on Kendo as well as shuji?"

"Sorry, no, I meant—"

"It's only a loss if I take it as such, it was a lesson, that way I grow. Your lesson may be to think before speaking."

"Well, thank you sensei." He didn't need to be chided by her anymore. Christ, he thought, she could blow hot and cold. "Your grandfather has asked for tea." The abruptness of his tone put her in her place. Peter turned and left. He could feel her eyes still spitting their poison at him. Rather than ignore her, he chose to turn and drink in his triumph. Sure enough she was watching him and he made to smile at his little glory of putting her in her place. His momentary victory was robbed from him and he was left standing like a fool by her simplest of bows. The utter serenity of the movement left him bereft of any haughtiness. There was no victory to be had for there was no game. He wandered back to where Thys was working.

THYS GLANCED at him picking up on his deflation. "So, will we get tea?"

"You might, very doubtful for me."

Thys almost fell to the floor with laughter, he couldn't help himself. After he sat down and was relatively composed he held his hands up at Peter. "I'm sorry. Sorry, Peter, really. She is too much like her grandmother and mother. I don't know if there is any of my DNA in her at all."

"No, it's fine, it's me."

"Bullshit! She's a tyrant." He took a moment to catch his breath and Peter stood awkwardly. Peter was mystified by his feelings for a girl who appeared willing to bite his head off. Thys could see it plainly on the young Dane's face. "But you know," Thys continued, his laughter only partially under control, "at least she's talking to you."

"For now, give it another five minutes."

"You owe me more than five minutes. Thief!" They both whirled to see Rie who had just approached with a tray of tea and some sweets. "He stole the azuki beans from my Kakigori, Grandpa."

"Yes, yes I have heard of this heinous crime."

"Don't take his side and make fun of it."

"Oh no, no, no." He held up his arms in submission. "The theft of red bean paste has started numerous wars."

"Funny," she playfully sneered at him and set the tray down. "Here's your tea. I have Kendo training now, I'll be back in a few hours." She came over and gave her grandfather a gentle, very un-Japanese, squeeze on his arm.

Thys rested his wrinkled hand on hers, "Remember Riechan, a falling leaf cannot force its own direction, it must allow flow, to achieve its path."

She thought a moment on what he said. Though he tried to portray himself as a 'country bumpkin type' his knowledge and wisdom contained a deep and rare understanding. "Thank you. Have you been talking to my kendo sensei?"

He held up his hands in mock protest. "Never, only my trees."

"Hmm, right." She didn't believe the old man for a second. He was far too well connected. Rie smiled at the old man and passed close to Peter on her way between the rows of miniature trees, up toward the house. Her proximity and the fragrance of her hair wafted through Peter. It seeped into his every pore, rifled his grey matter. It was as if nuerones, in a mental Mardi Gras, clattered in his head. He gazed after her. She stopped suddenly and he thought, hoped, she might turn. There was a long slow pause allowing the heat of the day to flush their cheeks. She resumed her walk to the house. Her hands were held tightly in front of her. The fingers squeezed tightly together, her knuckles went white. Rie wanted to turn and see him. She didn't know why, it was like kendo. She must hold her composure. To lose it would be a weakness.

Peter was disappointed she didn't turn to wave or smile – anything. Resigned he turned back to the bonsai trees. Thys, having seen the exchange, quickly lost himself in his tea to avoid embarrassing Peter again.

They resumed their ambient pace, each focused their attention to the trees. Peter, who was doing all the cleaning and lifting, was about to move a large old haggard looking Bonsai.

"Don't touch that!"

Peter jumped back at the harsh bark. "Sorry."

"No harm. I thought you knew this bonsai."

"No, no, I was just going to move it to clean around it."

"There are three special bonsai in the garden; the two up at the house and this one. They were given to me to care for and though the other older ones are doing well, this one is suffering. It has been in decline for years now. It has pride of place in my collection and yet it suffers. I am poor at caring for it."

"Why's it special?"

"Oh," the silver haired man toyed with the stone base of the miniature elm. "All bonsai are a bit like the owner – a reflection. One's bonsai can become the embodiment of the person. If one thinks that perception of the world is just a mirror of one's true soul, then the bonsai embodies the soul of the person in a miniature time."

"Whoa. More than just trees."

"Everything is more than it seems, if one looks in a different angle."

"I thought Rie was my only challenge, it seems even the trees are out to kick my ass."

"Ha! We should all be so lucky as to know when we need to be kicked."

"I'm sure Rie's kick will come like a lightning bolt from the blue."

"I'm sure it will."

"So who's the soul reflected in this bonsai?"

Thys shifted and reached for his tea. The cup was from a set by one of Japan's esteemed potters. They were wholly unique. He turned the cup in his hands, hesitant to speak. With a sigh he refilled the cast iron teapot from the small pump flask, swirled it a few moments and gently topped up his cup. He refreshed Peter's as well. He waved Peter to a small wooden stool, grayed with age.

Peter thought everything about Thys had a timeless, sage-type quality; from the bonsai and kendo, to his stately Minka-style home, and his Ashikaga wife. After studying Japanese language for six years, he felt like a child standing on the beach with the vastness of the ocean before him.

"It belongs to Emperor Hirohito. Shortly before he passed away, he first asked Chieko if she would object to the idea, she said 'no' of course. Then he approached me and asked me to care for it. I was invited to tea at the palace. It was late October and he had been ill for a long time. It was such a pleasure to see him, but he was not in a good state. I told him of some marine journals I had read recently and he showed genuine interest. Even though he was so ill, he still had a tremendous fascination for nature. Our tea together was brief and he made his request. I was humbled that he should ask that I tend this esteemed personal object. Even more so to pay so high a respect to Chieko, by asking her permission. It was a most un-Japanese thing to do. He was always a contradiction. Chieko was humbled and that is no small thing for an Ashikaga woman. It was the highest respect to pay her. I will forever be grateful to him for that, among many things."

"I've heard Mrs. Rasmussen is of noble ancestry."

"That depends how you look at it. It is both noble and ignoble. The northern Imperial line, which exists today, was put in place originally by Ashikaga Takauji. Takauji fought to establish his family's shogun rule that lasted for nearly two and a half centuries. So in many ways he was a monumental figure in history. But the Japanese hate him because he betrayed their greatest hero Kusunoki Masashige, who was abandoned on the banks of Minato River. Ashikaga was a traitor to his one time friend and that takes a long time to forget in any culture." Thys spoke slowly focusing on the steam wafting over the brim of the teacup. "Man can forgive a crime, an error, but betrayal of honor, is an act never to know forgiveness. There is no redemption. Hirohito was acutely aware of that. The betrayal of honor is a most haunting affliction. "

"So, Emperor Hirohito brought his bonsai here for you to care for?"

"Yes, well, had them brought. He was very insistent on it. Over our years together we spent several lovely afternoons in this garden. Usually however, our visits were within the palace gardens – it was easier for security. When he joined us here, he would arrive in private escort and we would sit and discuss various scientific journals or occasionally news articles. Chieko served him. It was a huge honor for us both, but that doesn't matter, it's a private matter." Thys glanced at his watch. "Good Lord, I'll be late. That's what happens among bonsai – time condenses. I'll be gone until about six. Could you trim the pathways, rake the gardens and repack the soil and rocks around the new pond on your own? I don't know where Shimoda is today."

"Of course."

"It's a lot to do, sorry."

"Without Rie here, it'll be safe. I won't have to fear getting thumped."

"Thank you, Peter."

The old man ambled up to the house. Having recalled the passing of his friend, Thys' spirit, like a wilting, sun-drenched flower, drooped. Peter watched the saddened figure drift toward the stately, ash-colored house. The house was a grand structure in the Japanese wooden Minka style. Thys had told him that after the war the Ashikaga family, who were reluctant to allow her marriage to a foreigner, even if he spoke Japanese, wanted to have a suitable home for their daughter and a modern home was an anathema to their taste. The family, which still held huge tracts of land in the countryside, dissembled this two hundred year old traditional home in the countryside and re-erected it here on a site that was burnt out from the air raids. The age and grandeur of the place rivaled any new building in Tokyo. Even today it was so revered in Tokyo that Japanese and foreign tourists alike, passed by daily and took pictures of the massive beams and eloquent tiered structure.

***

IT WAS NEARING three when he at last finished the paths. With temperatures in the mid thirties it was a scorching day to be working a shovel. All he had left to do was to pack the soil around the pond edge and relay the flat slate rocks on the pond perimeter, and he would be finished for the day. As

it wouldn't require any great aesthetic he had been allowed
to do it. No doubt Shimoda would find fault with it, but so
what, he hadn't appeared today. As Peter was alone, he
thought he could turn on his old CD player; another
sayonara sale purchase. With the portable unit, he could
enjoy some music while he shoveled. He took his shirt off,
got the music blaring, and gamely tackled the mound of dirt.
Within half an hour the dirt was packed down and he had
begun to haul and lay the heavy, awkward slabs of rock. The
little CD unit was blaring out Queen's, 'The Show Must Go
On' when it suddenly died in mid phrase. Peter dropped the
flat seventy-five pound rock he was carrying and ambled,
somewhat exhausted, over to the veranda edge where the
unit was leaning against the wall and tried the 'play' button
again. It fired into life and he resumed his hauling. He
needed the music to keep him energized for the last of the
rocks. 'Bohemian Rhapsody', one of his all-time favorite
Queen tunes, was half way through when it again went
dead. He was annoyed and turned to go and restart the little
unit. He stopped and leaned on his shovel. He had found the
trouble or she had found it, depending on the point of view.

"Ikebana and Queen do not harmonize," Rie said
plainly.

"And the Ikebana is where?" He was not about to be
bullied again no matter how gorgeous the bully may be.
"Not on the end of my shovel. Unless you see yourself as
some sort of ass kicking flower."

"I thought the Danish understood minimalism."

"Yes, but shutting off Queen is more like vandalism."

"I'm trying to do some ikebana over here for my grandmother, do you mind?"

Peter was taken aback by her snotty-nosed attitude. She

was upset about something, but it wasn't his problem. "No, not at all. I'm trying to do some gardening for your grandfather, do you mind? All you had to do was ask. Christ I would've been happy to shut it off." Peter crossed over to her and snatched the CD player out of her hand. He walked back to the pond and his work. "Politeness seems to have been lost on you." He muttered to himself.

"Sorry, I didn't hear that. What were you muttering? If you're a man say it to my face."

"I said," he turned his tired body to face her square on. "Politeness seems to be lost on you." Peter paused and then a much more conciliatory tone washed from him. "And I can't understand it because you're very—"

"What?" She interrupted harshly.

What was happening here he wondered? "Nothing, forget it, sorry about the tunes." He turned back to the shovel and tried to lose himself in the work. This was all going so badly. When he was bent over to take another stone, he noticed the white tabi and geta sandals directly in front of him. He looked up. The luscious spitting eyes were staring at him.

"So very what?"

"Nothing, forget it. Christ, Thys was right."

"About what?"

"Nothing, look, forget it. I'm not here. You do your ikebana. I'll shovel. Ok?"

"Ok! You happy?!"

"Yeah, ok?!"

"Ok!" She turned and strutted back to the veranda. She walked up along and around the corner to where she must've been working. Stillness resumed and he lost himself on the end of the shovel. She was so frustrating to him. He'd known her only a few days and his brain was punch drunk with angst and desire.

AFTER ANOTHER HOUR of hard shoveling and carrying of ridiculously heavy rocks, Peter was dying for a drink of water. He knew he would have to ask her. He refused to do that. He could get one as soon as he finished – another fifteen minutes. Once he was finished shoveling, he could just slip out of the back yard, after putting the tools away in the rear shed. He wouldn't have to see her. There was a vending machine about a hundred yards down the road. After a few cans of Pocari Sweat sport drink, he could walk back and pick up his scooter from the front of the house. He could avoid her completely.

Happy with the way the slab laying turned out, he scattered white rock among the slabs and he was finished. Peter loaded the shovels into the wheelbarrow, picked up the CD Player and his shirt, then with everything loaded in the barrow, he headed for the back of the yard. As he passed the room where she would be working, he focused his eyes forward refusing to look at her. Peter was about five steps past her, when he heard her. It was a soft, whisper of his name. He had wanted to hear it so very badly, he was worried he might of imagined it. He paused with his back to her as she had earlier. He didn't look back. He was just about to heave the barrow and start again.

"Pete?" It was a stronger voice and she said Pete not Peter. He put the wheelbarrow down. She was kneeling on the edge of the veranda. "Would you like some oolong tea? It's nice and cold. You must be very thirsty. You've worked like a demon."

He was desperate to go up and see her. He could just

make out part of the ikebana behind her. Everything around her was serenity and beauty, yet when they came near each other it was like petrol and a match. He should leave it. "I'm fine, thank you." He turned.

"You have to." He turned back with a look of disdain on his face. "Please, if grandmother finds out I've not done what she said, I'll be skewered like a yakitori."

"Well, that's not a bad image. From temple to temple, or to keep your lips closed."

"Very funny." She held the glass out to him. "Here."

The soft tone crippled his aloof intentions. He crossed back up to her and took the glass. He downed it in one go. She watched his long lanky torso as the cool brown tea was gulped down. She could imagine it swirl in his chest, around his pectorals and lower to his belt line. She glanced up – he was watching her stare at his body! "Would, would, you like some, ah, some more?"

"Yes, please. May I see your ikebana arrangement?"

She was surprised, but pleased. "Yeah, of course." Rie turned away, she was happy to get out of his sight after having been caught staring at him. She shifted to the side while pouring a second glass. He leaned past her. She could smell his sweat and manliness. His shoulder muscles glistened.

"Wow! God that's amazing. To say so much with so little. Is there a theme or statement, or is it wrong to ask?" He straightened and looked down at the creature kneeling before him. He thought she was far more captivating than the flower arrangement. They had such a great time chatting together before, how could it blow so hot and cold? He thought an apology might set things straight. "I'm sorry about the music, I never knew you were here."

"It's okay, I shouldn't have snapped, but I got told off again by my kendo sensei. I was in a bad mood, sorry."

"So, we're even?"

"Except for the Kakigori."

"Jesus!" He took another drink and waved toward the ikebana with his glass. "Is there a theme?"

"Well, it's not' Fat Bottomed Girls' by Queen," she said.

"Pity. Good song." She nodded in agreement and threw her hair back across her shoulder unconsciously.

"Sometimes dissecting artwork is not appropriate. Sometimes you have to be with it for a while to fully articulate or find what it means. My New York art instructors think that's a cop out."

"What's the theory, 'for every action there is an equal and opposite critic?'" Peter sat on the edge of the veranda and sipped the tea. It was hot and the sound of cicada reverberated across the garden. The heat stilled the garden, lured it to sleep.

Rie was unsure how to begin her next request. She knew she had to, wanted to really, but things between them were still fragile at best. "Pete, my ah... grandmother, she... she also insisted that I treat that mess on your back."

"What? No, it's fine."

"She told me to. You know what she's like."

"I know what you are like and you're liable to put salt in it."

She bit her lower lip. It was a way to keep her attitude in check. Her grandmother had suggested a nip of her lower lip would give her a moment to think rather than react. "Come on you'll get an infection. I'll wash it with antiseptic and then put this cream on and you can shower in a couple hours after it's absorbed. My grandmother left the stuff here, so I have to do it."

"I've seen you in Kendo, do you know the word gentle?" The moment he said the last word he wished he could take it back. It was a spike at her, an unnecessary jab. She had obviously been seen as a hard woman, even though she was only his age.

"I'm not really a bitch, you know."

"Sorry. But if you scream 'KEEAA' and stamp your foot – I'm out the door."

She smiled and touched his bare shoulder to turn his back to her. The touch made a possibility shiver deep inside them. "Okay, Viking, this will sting."

He dared not flinch at the touch of her hand. She would no doubt think it was a weakness. The stinging was like a party of wasps having a tribal dance on the welt. At least it passed in about three minutes.

"You can relax your teeth now. You clench them any tighter, you'll be going to a dentist next."

"Very funny. I think you enjoyed seeing my pain."

"Doesn't count as part payment for the theft."

"God, girl, let it go." She laughed and slid around to face him. It was at that point that he saw the inside of her collar. A welt about ten centimeters long was right on her collarbone. "What happened to your neck?"

She covered it immediately and stood up. "I had a lesson today, my mistake."

She went very cold to him. He shouldn't have been looking at her so closely. He didn't understand her, but he realized she had decided it was time for him to leave. "Well, we all make them, I did too today." He had a plan yet wasn't sure he had the balls to carry it out. "I learn from my lessons and… as I ah… also have an outstanding debt." She said nothing just stared straight at him. There was such a formidable challenge in her eyes. He was convinced it was a mistake to ask. *What the hell,* he thought. "Will you have dinner with me tonight?"

"No."

"Oh," she said nothing else. She stared at him making him squirm in embarrassment. "Just no?"

"Uhm. I can't, I am eating with my grandparents."

"Of course, yes. Well, maybe I'll see you tomorrow then?"

"Don't ah... Well." Rie was surprised he had given up so quickly. She wanted him to show interest in her... of course ... but wasn't really ready... if he actually did. She hadn't thought that far ahead. "I, I'm meeting some of my high school friends at a jazz bar in Tamachi later, around ten, if you're free. It's called the Snooze Blues. One of my class-mates is on trumpet. He's really good. It's not Queen."

"I'd love to go." He was about to leave when she touched his elbow lightly. He turned and she realized it had been an unconscious action.

"Ah," she was panicked. She was kneeling and he stood bare-chested over her. He was very attractive in a George Michael-Viking-Robert Redford kind of way. She wasn't sure that mix was even possible. It didn't matter; he was standing over her. "Make sure you leave it a couple hours before showering. But do shower cause you're sweaty and stink."

"Tousind Tak," she looked at him puzzled, "a thousand thanks in Danish." He turned and left out the back gate.

The ride home on the scooter was a vague drift on a sea of meaningless traffic. The welt across his back felt wonder-ful. It was still stiff, but where she had touched was, well – she had touched him!

***

THE MOMENT he walked in Peter wondered if there was ever a jazz bar without people in dark sunglasses, in a dark room, smoking bucket loads of cigarettes. Peter had intentionally arrived late to avoid any awkwardness and didn't want to look too keen, though he certainly was. In the short time he had been in Tokyo, his nights out had consisted of Roppongi nightclubs, where foreigners were usually avoided by all but the sleazy girls or drunk morons. Anyone with half a brain could sleep with any drunk little girl in a love motel. To him the clubs were just too much of a waste of time. He inevitably ended up leaving clubs early and cruising around a few of the smaller pubs. Most of the guys he knew had been in Japan quite some time and were fixed up with long-term girlfriends or playing the market so hard, it was one 'shag' after another. In either situation, his nights out had been less than fulfilling.

He picked Rie out in a moment. His eyes just naturally gravitated to the being in the corner. She stood out, somehow apart from everyone else. She didn't do anything or say anything unusual, she was just chilling to the music. She hadn't seen him enter and he watched her from the side of the room. His eyes just filled with her, he could feel the swirl in his mind, her arms around his waist her body on the back of the bike, her hands gently rubbing cream onto his back. Then there were other moments. He was so stupid; a pathetic puppy. Peter thought about how he was behaving and how he had fallen blindly for someone so tempestuous. He began to think he was reading far too much into this girl. The last thing he needed was to irritate one of the most

prestigious lecturers at Sophia University by fooling around
with his granddaughter. He considered leaving. He could
just make an excuse. He could say his back hurt or the bike
broke down. The band finished their number and he
slipped out. He hadn't been seen.

He waited at the tiny four-person elevator, but it was
taking forever and he wanted a quick get away, so he took
the six flights down to the street where he'd left his scooter.

Peter stood in front of his scooter and halfheartedly
searched for his keys. He didn't really want to go; but staying
was awkward and the band would be finished soon, he'd left
it too late, she'd be going home soon. He looked up trying to
decide what to do. There was a sharp knocking on the back
of his helmet. He turned around and there she was. There
were those eyes, even in the night they slashed into his
mind, muddying his thoughts.

"Hi ya. Thanks for coming."

"Oh yeah." He took the helmet off again.

"My friends are all looking forward to meeting you.
They can't believe the dragon invited somebody out. Guess
I do have a reputation." She smiled at him and wrapped
her arm around his. Peter felt his resolve melting. She
leaned in close to him, "Mmm you smell so much better
than this afternoon." Peter could only smile at her eyes.
She had obviously had a few drinks and held him quite
close. His mind was tingling with her being so close. He
could feel the side of her breast press against his forearm.
He was not paying attention to the trip back to the jazz bar.
It slipped by in a haze. She was speaking he was nodding.
She was so close to him. He thought he could feel her
breath. They re-entered the jazz bar and several heads
turned and waved them over. Peter suddenly felt like Al
Pacino in the Godfather when he was thunderstruck with

love. Who was in control? Who was the puppet and who pulling the strings? He didn't really care, he was happy. Peter shook hands with her friends. They were a welcoming bunch. They made space at the table and one of the guys poured him a beer.

The jazz was good. Very good. The company was an eclectic mix of artists and entrepreneurs. Peter was the only academic in the group.

After the band finished its last set, the trumpet player came over and joined them. He shook everyone's hand and in an oddly Western way, kissed Rie on the cheek. It wasn't passionate, very European in fact. Jealousy blasted through Peter's eyes like a hurricane. How could she be so casual with this musician and yet treat him like some leper? What he wouldn't do to kiss those lips.

"You're not American?" The trumpet player asked interrupting Peter's thoughts.

"No, Danish."

"Ah, so we won't be able to show you how jazz should be played."

"I thought Jazz came from Louisiana, the South?" Peter said.

"Came from there, but found its life here."

"Really? Wow better not tell Miles Davis or Charlie Parker."

"It's growing here," said another of her friends, in sunglasses and a 70s white 'Bee Gees' suit.

"What he means is, like everything in Japan, we take something and make it better," Rei added.

"Do you really?" Peter asked.

"The West comes up with ideas, but we are the people that improve them," the trumpet player said.

Peter didn't want to be difficult, but wasn't prepared to

have opinions shoveled at him as if he had to accept them. "So, why is Rie so caught up in her Japanese culture?"

"I'm not caught up in it. It's part of me." Rie stood up and was now just over eye to eye with the tall but seated Dane.

"So you're not drinking in the evil Western ways? Not making them better in your unique way."

"Why would I? I mean at least I know my culture. At least I have one."

That pissed him off and he stood up over the little woman. "What? So the Danish don't?"

"Can you name anything Danish?"

"I certainly can and I don't have to go to the States to try to get something and import it. We are a proud people." Peter was getting riled too.

"Then why are you here speaking Japanese?"

"Why are you in the States studying art? Why did you copy jazz? Why aren't you off plucking your koto?"

"You're arrogant." Rie poked him hard in the chest.

"Me! You're arrogant!" He pointed his finger right at the luscious eyes he yearned for. "I never suggested you didn't have any culture. You always go out of your way to insult everything about me and my culture and your grandfather's."

"He's more Japanese than Danish!" Rie yelled at Peter.

"It's so nice to have her back from the States," said the white suited friend.

"I bet they're happy she's back here too," the trumpet player added.

"Safer for them."

"Are you two finished scrapping?" the trumpeter asked calmly.

"Could be your grandfather's more Japanese than you?" Peter leaned right into Rie's face. "You've been raised in a soulless international school and grasp at straws of culture to find out who you are."

"You're looking for real culture to explain away your dissatisfaction with yourself. Therefore you try to assume others." She spat the words like poison.

"Look who speaks English."

"Yeah and who speaks Japanese and doesn't know shit all about the people."

"At least I know who I am and not some prissy, spoiled, international school tart."

The slap across his face finished his sentence and she was gone. The entire jazz bar had fallen to silence as their exchange rifled back and forth. Peter looked around at the array of glowing cigarette ends and reflective sunglasses.

The trumpeter spoke up. "Peter, she really likes you. That is the first time she has cared enough to smack someone."

"Gee, thanks."

"Thank you." The white suit laughed. "Usually she has a go at us." They all laughed. "Better go see how she is. Be careful there are two sides to that girl. You never know which one is coming up." They all laughed again and waved him off to follow her.

Peter didn't want to go and see her, but at the same time was worried about her being so upset. He didn't really mean all he had said. She just sort of made him fly off. He waved to the friends and slipped out and down the stairs.

He jumped on his scooter and headed toward the station. There was only one main route to the station and he knew he would find her either picking up a cab or taking the last subway home.

She was only about three blocks from the jazz bar and he pulled up and jumped off the scooter. She was walking quickly with her head down. Peter couldn't tell if she was brooding or crying. He ran up beside her and pulled her arm back.

"Rie, please, wait."

"You! What the hell do you want?" Rie snarled.

"I, I just want to —"

"What? Spew a few more insults you didn't spit out in front of my friends? Why'd I think you could ever be... something?"

"Look, you don't have to go on the attack all the time. I'm not out to hurt you."

"Fooled me. You spent your time trying to make me look small."

"You were insulting me." He shook his head. It wasn't working. "You're wrong. You know, maybe you are a bitch, like you even said."

It was the other cheek that took the smack this time. She turned and strutted away. In two steps he was behind her and whirled her around. He caught her arms as she spun and pinned them behind her. He kissed her hard on the lips and for a moment she responded. He felt the lips go soft and succulent, her body softened against him, her womanly shape melted on him, but only for an instant. Her body slipped down and she spun out of his arms and shoved him away.

"What? You think you can force me? You think I'm some kind of prize?"

"What and I'm some kind of slap me toy?" She turned and strutted away. She had a lovely irresistible movement in her hips but her body was a force of menace. He called after her. "Don't think this beating will be offered to clear my debt." He thought he detected the hint of a pause in her step, but she continued into the subway.

Was this a game, he wondered? She turned into the subway station and was gone. Was tonight a draw? At least both sides of his face stung. Nothing like symmetry, though that wasn't very Japanese. He rubbed the cheek. It stung. She could throw a really good smack. No doubt she had lots of experience. He went back to his scooter, hopped on and drove home. The taste of her lipstick lingered in his mind. The sting of her passion lingered on his cheeks.

5

Perhaps it was because both sides of his face were evenly matched that no one in his class noticed the bruises on his cheeks. They weren't serious, but the end of each finger was quite clear just below his eye line. She packed quite a slap; open palmed and stinging. That morning the professors had taken it upon themselves to unload excessive amounts of reading on the dozen post grad students, and he was not looking forward to the next three weeks of research and page flipping. His first thought was that it would mean less time with Rie. Though he had to be realistic, it was very unlikely that would happen, so in truth the reading was a Godsend.

With Rie, he would have to do some serious pleading to be seen as anything other than a cockroach to step on. Hopefully she wouldn't mention their squabble to Thys. It was a privilege to be offered the position to work alongside him and not one that should be cast away over a little love spat. It wasn't a love spat – it was a quarrel. The love was not there. At least it wasn't in the open.

Peter parked his scooter outside and was about to knock

on the front door when it rumbled open. Thys and Chieko stood before him. Thys wore a formal black tuxedo with traditional white silk tie. Chieko left him speechless. Attired in a stunning black and purple kimono with gold obi she looked as if she had walked off a magazine page. Peter stared stupidly. He recognized the Ashikaga family crest clearly indicated on the collar and sleeves. They were heading out.

"Ah, Peter. What luck, I caught you before we left. We are off to a wedding for a few days," Thys said.

"Sorry I'm late. The Profs have decided to drown us in ancient texts."

"Lovely for you. Maybe, eh?"

"You've had some lunch, Peter?" Chieko asked. He looked at her again and couldn't believe the magazine cover could speak. "Peter?"

"You look absolutely stunning. I have never seen—"

She waved him quiet. "That's very kind Peter, but have you had some lunch?"

"No, but that's fine, thank you." He was still a bit dazed by the vision before him. Chieko turned back into the house. From behind Peter saw that her obi was tied in the shape of a gold and purple butterfly, he was gobsmacked.

Thys was amused by Peter's reaction. Chieko often left men, both foreign and Japanese speechless, and that was just with her looks, not her attitude. "I've left a list of instructions with Rie to help you through the afternoon. Shimodasan said he will not be able to assist today until later, so you are on your own, but Rie is there if you need help."

"I'm sure I'll be fine."

"Just ask her." He patted the tall Dane's shoulder. "You know she is quite a powerful little bundle."

Panic crossed Peter's eyes at the thought that she had

come home and revealed their argument to the older couple. The door slid open and Chieko stepped out. She lightly touched Peter's arm.

"I've told Rie to make you some lunch. No guarantees on the preparation, but she won't kill you. Well, not yet."

There it was again. Did they know and were making fun of him?

Thys laughed out loud. "She did put one of her high school sweethearts in hospital for a week with mussels she'd supposedly cooked."

"That's not fair Thys. It was an accident. You now what mussels are like."

"An accident. You think?" Thys continued to laugh.

Rie called from inside. "I can hear you." The door rumbled open. She looked at her grandfather. "He'll get what he's given. Whether Peter survives or not is not up to me." She rolled the door closed. Peter glanced up as the door rumbled and thought he saw her glance at him just before it closed, but he couldn't be sure.

Thys raised his eyebrows at Peter and whispered "God hath no wrath like a woman scorned."

"Come on Thys, we'll be late. Peter, looks as if you've got sunburn on your cheeks, both of them. There is some cream inside."

Was there a smile? Peter wasn't sure.

Chieko led the older man away. "I'll be back late tomorrow, Thys may stay an extra day." They crossed away to the waiting black Toyota Crown sedan. He waved them off. A heavy thundering sigh escaped his chest. What a remarkable woman Mrs. Rasmussen was.

Peter was left at the front door, unsure of how to enter and aware she might be waiting on the other side of the door to blast him again. She may have gone further into the house and might refuse to open the door to humiliate him and force him to walk around.

Humility would win over valor and he elected to walk all the way around and come in at the foot of the garden. He would be nearer the tools anyway.

Rie stood just to the left of the door and watched him through the crack in the shutters. He was so polite and respectful to her grandparents, she couldn't understand why he picked a fight with her constantly. She waited. His fine features were tanned from the garden work, but she could distinctly see the finger marks below his eye on the right cheek. It was her first slap and was much better released. She hoped the other side wasn't as bad. Then again he deserved it, sort of. He stood lost and it looked as if he might leave all together. Rie touched her lips unconsciously; a memory tingled in them. His lips felt as if still there; hot and powerful, so very powerful. She was about to reach for the door when he walked away. He must be coming in the back. She dashed to the veranda and opened up her art texts. She would look disinterested in him.

Peter made his way through the garden with the wheelbarrow of tools. He could see she was on the porch. She was wearing tight jeans and a white loose fitting men's shirt. Her long mane of hair was clipped back. She was absorbed in a book so he thought he would slink through to the other side before starting the filling of the fishpond. The greater the distance between them the better. He pushed the wheelbarrow silently past her.

"Hello." He was about three meters past when she'd called out.

He stopped and turned to her. "Hi ya." He waited but she stayed stuck in her book. He realized she had intentionally greeted him just to ignore him. He looked at her body laying face down. Her jeans were tight and her body very shapely. He had never really looked at her body that much, as he was usually dissolved by her eyes. Now however they were stuck in a book and he didn't exist. He turned away and took a trimmer from the wheelbarrow.

"What time do you want lunch? Gran has told me to make a meal for you. I think she's being rash, but, whatever."

"No, thank you, that's fine. I don't want anything."

"She has told me to, so I will. Believe me it's not what I want to do."

"No, that's obvious."

"What does that mean?"

"Just that you don't want to, that's all."

"Right, another snide comment."

"No, really Rie. I don't want anything from you, any lunch I mean, and … and that's all it means. It's clear you don't want to see or talk to me, much less cook for me. I don't know if I blame you or not, but there it is. I'll pick up some rice cakes at the convenience store later."

"Fine. You'll get nothing from me."

He shook his head at the girl he had somehow begun to fall in love with between battles. He was normally confident around women, but just looking at her turned his mind delusional. It was as if each time he looked at her some being put his brain into an older wringer washer and wrung it through the rollers then rinsed and repeated. He didn't know if he was coming or going, but in honesty, he was enthralled by her. He shook his head – he had to escape the wringer washer syndrome. "I don't know how last night happened, but I'm sorry it turned out the way it did. But thank you, the jazz was very good. I'm sorry about the end bit, the ah… "

She turned to him. The top two buttons of her shirt were undone and the purple bruise on her collarbone was clear to see. It stood off her skin like a rose against snow. Before the close of her shirt he could just see the fullness of her chest begin. She was about to speak, but before she could utter a word, he turned away and moved quickly up the path. Peter had decided not to trust his mouth or his brain in her presence.

There were two small jobs to do before the actual filling of the pond could happen. He had to trim some bushes back and then sink the water lines that fed and drained the system. After those two jobs were done all he had to do was wash the pond before filling it. Then Thys could acquire his beloved carp for his this virtual lake. It wasn't deep but it certainly was huge. It would take a lot of carp to fill.

With a bucket and brush he scrubbed each crevice and rock surface of the floor and walls of the pond. It was hot dirty work and he had been at it for two hours before he was finally able to straighten his back and rinse his hands. He knew she had been watching for some time and the book was just a ploy. He stepped out of the large pond and began hosing the dirty water down. He flicked on a submerged sump pump to drain the water and in a few minutes the forty square meter pond was clean.

Peter went to the rear and turned on the water feed as well as a garden hose to fill the massive area, it would take at least a few hours. He watched the water flow into the pond. He was tired and would have a long evening of study ahead of him.

"Peter?" It was the first time Rie had spoken to him in hours, even though she was no more than five meters away. She had sat or sprawled out to read on the tatami mat near the edge of the veranda the whole time. He had often stolen glances at her body and visions of it toyed with his heart rate.

Rie had been reading – well facing the book anyway. A lot of her time was spent daydreaming about the tall blond man in front of her. She would glance up and have silent conversations with him, even though he was hunched over scrubbing like a demon. The way he attacked the work it was obvious he wanted to leave as quickly as possible, to get away from her. Rie remembered how her parents used to sit for hours and talk with her grandparents about all manner of things. They were scientists too and spent so much time in the field that she had been half raised by her grandparents. She was close to her family, it had been hard to leave and go to university in New York. That was why she had a hard shell around her, at least that was what other people said. Then again her grandmother said it was just an over abundance of Ashikaga pride.

She looked up and he was standing looking at her. She'd forgotten she called his name. She scrambled to her feet and pulled her shirt straight. She found herself unconsciously arranging her hair. Why? She felt nervous and expectant. "Do you want something to eat? I know you love Taiyaki, I bought some and ah… and there is fruit and rice cakes with pickled plum. Or I could make some noodles – hot or cold which ever you like." She was surprised at how warm her voice sounded.

He hesitated to answer. He was actually starving and didn't fancy the two-block walk to the convenience store, but then he didn't want a fight over this or anything else.

"Regardless of what my grandfather said, I won't poison you. How much poison can I put in fresh fruit?" A giggle of nervousness erupted from her and she hated it. She thought it made her seem weak. In all honesty she was feeling vulnerable. Would she get another rejection? If so she'd be ready for it.

"I, uh, I don't know and I'm not sure I could answer properly. Just some water would be fine. I'll go to the store. In fact, forget the water, I'll be back in twenty minutes."

"Come on. Peter." She swallowed hard to keep her focus and took a deep breath. "I know you don't want me to do anything but, ah, I wouldn't mind. I mean it won't be much. I usually cook student food, which is the family joke. My parents don't eat anything I make. In fact, I think I am the only one who does."

"Well, I have hours to kill while this lake fills... how about I cook for you? It's kind of a skill I have. I can whip up passable food out of nothing. I'll raid your Gran's fridge. What do you say?"

"But I wanted—"

"I have a debt. You study, I'll cook. If you like it — we're even, deal?"

Rie held out her hand to help him up onto the veranda. "Deal."

Whipping up a meal was easy for Peter when he opened the fridge. It was a cornucopia of delights. Being a formally trained housewife and lady of culture, Chieko's stores were exquisite. Peter quickly cooked off some noodles, cooled them down and iced them. Rie hovered around and he shooed her away to study; it was, after all, his debt. Plus he wanted to surprise her and win some points back.

He sautéed a few handfuls of crayfish along with some fresh herbs and pesto. In a matter of minutes he had a cold seafood pasta prepped. He sliced a fresh mango and sprinkled pieces on top as an exotic finish. It would pass.

He slid the door back to the front tatami room and placed the two plates on the low central table. He went back

and got some tea and the lone Taiyaki, which he had cut.
She hadn't stirred and was obviously asleep. He crept beside
her and listened to her breathing. It was soft, gentle. He
touched her shoulder and shook her. She raised her head
and smiled up at him through a cascade of hair.

"Sorry, I fell asleep."

"No problem, lunch is ready. Apart from the book crease
across your face, everything is fine."

"Oh God. You see me at the worst of times; fighting,
bruised, bitchy, crying; no wonder you don't want to have
lunch with me."

"Rie just eat. I hope you like it. We'll share the Taiyaki."

"Don't worry, I'll check how fairly it's been cut." She
grinned at him and he could feel his mind blurring to mush.
It was heading for the wringer washer again.

LUNCH WAS WONDERFULLY civil and they spent at least an
hour discussing the books she had strewn across the floor.
Her laughter filled the garden. They were just about to share
the Taiyaki pastry for dessert when an eruption came from
the pond. One of the pressure supply hoses must have burst
and was spewing a fountain of water across the garden and
striking the veranda. Rie scrambled to cover the books while
Peter went to shut off the supply.

He waded into the pond, now a foot deep, and reached
down to locate the hose. He reattached it and tightened it
down.

"Turn the tap on, Rie."

"Okay." She twisted the tap on full and crossed over to
the edge of the pond. She watched as Peter leaned down
and checked the fitting.

"It's tight now. Maybe I didn't secure it properly before."

Just as he reached for the tools he was hit with a mass of water. This time it wasn't a leak. It was Rie. She'd turned the garden hose on him. He tried to splash back but was getting drenched. She jumped out of the pond and made for the veranda but he beat her there and she was forced to run down the garden. He was right behind her. She ran through the rows of bonsai trees and cut the corner near Hirohito's elm. Her hip caught a lower loose brick and the bonsai spun, about to topple. Peter caught it and shoved it roughly back into place. He was now only a meter from Rie, who continued her escape. He reached out and caught the waist of her jeans. He squeezed tight and clamped down on the belt loop. He pulled her back and wrapped her in his arms from behind. Rie struggled and kicked but with his arms wrapped around her waist he easily lifted her off the ground and marched her up the path.

"Now I got you."

"Let me go. Peter!"

"Splash me will you."

She saw what he was about to do as they approached the pond. "No, no, please Peter. This is a favorite shirt. Please don't." Peter was just laughing as she struggled. He was at the edge of the pond. He spun the little body in his arms and in one motion tossed her flat into the pond of murky water.

She struggled to her feet and slipped falling again. Her hair was straggled all over her face. "You bastard!"

"Now, now, language."

"God, I hate you." She waded to the edge of the pool. With the clinging shirt hugging her body, he was able to have a clear view of how sexy her body was. "What are you staring at?"

He could say nothing, only smile. She had a lovely body.

"Jerk."

"You started it."

"Piss off." She stepped up onto the veranda and water drained from the bottoms of her jeans. "Christ!" She was pulling her shirt from her skin. "Why do you make me angry? I don't want to hate you. I don't, really want to." She had begun to stifle a cry and was gulping air. "I, I really want … shit." She was through he door and he could hear her feet stamping up the stairs. She was crying. He'd gone too far. He should've never looked at her, that was the invasion, not the toss in the water.

"Ah, shit, shit." He'd blown it. The one thing he wanted was raging in a cloud of smoke. Why was every moment together a firecracker of misguided confusion? He remembered the damaged bonsai wall and wandered back to investigate.

When Rie had gone around the corner she must have hit the top supporting brick and twisted it out of place. Peter hadn't put it back at all well. Holding the base he twisted the bricks to realign the base. The bricks had to be cleared of debris before they would align, but it wasn't a big job. In truth he was more distracted listening to shear if Rie was coming. The base of the bonsai itself swiveled very easy, as if hinged. He had thought it was one cement piece, but the lower base was actually hollow. There was a book inside, a diary. He pulled it out leaving the top of the bonsai base open.

He turned the book over and opened to the first page. A tingle crossed his face like dancing Novocain. The book grew heavy in his hands as the sense of trouble, which would be associated with it, crept across his mind. From the dust on the cover and the secreted hiding place it was obvious he had been the first to uncover it. If he didn't have enough hassles with the granddaughter he now had this to deal with. Could he keep it? Shimoda's glowering face flashed across his face and the warning not to mess with things he didn't understand. He turned another page.

The chrysanthemum crest and date 1985 -1989, clearly spelled trouble. He had stumbled on to Hirohito's last diary. That was why the emperor had insisted on Thys keeping the bonsai. The Emperor's final thoughts were entrusted to his friend.

Peter leafed randomly through the old book. What thoughts were contained? The writing was very stylized and the language archaic. He was only understanding every third or fourth symbol. Would the book describe his decision to surrender, his opinions of McArthur or Japan, or even himself? Would his last thoughts condemn the Japanese military that threw the country into war? Would it condemn himself? Why was it hidden?

The latch of the gate opened and closed. He looked up to see Shimoda. Shimoda distilled the significance of the book in moments. With Peter standing before the revered bonsai, its base open, holding the book with the chrysanthemum emblazoned, it was clear they both knew the importance of the book in Peter's hand. The open secret cavity below Hirohito's elm left nothing in doubt. But this belonged to Thys, Peter thought, not some half-baked radical idiot.

"What's that?"

"Nothing."

"That is the Emperor's. Give it to me. It belongs to Japan."

"It belongs to Thys. You want it for your sick group."

"Give it to me. It is for the Japanese people. Give it to me, you foreign pig." Shimoda lunged for the book and they crashed into a table of bonsai. Shimoda had one hand on Peter's throat and the other grasped at Peter's left arm that kept the diary from the shorter Shimoda's grasp. Shimoda spun and threw Peter against another table of bonsai that toppled with a crash. Peter was stunned by the violence and passion that spewed from Shimoda. It made him want to keep it from the radical bastard even more. Shimoda's powerful gardener fingers grabbed Peter from behind and his nails dug deep into the back of Peter's neck. Before Peter could react he felt his head propelled through the air as his head slammed against the side panel of the bonsai shelf. Peter's left eyebrow split open. Warm blood trickled into his vision. Still he clasped the book out of Shimoda's reach. "That is mine. I know what is best. The Japanese must know the Emperor's thoughts. Give it to me." Shimoda punched Peter high under the outstretched arm causing him to buckle forward. Shimoda went for the book but Peter whipped up and head butted Shimoda's nose. It broke cleanly. Struggling to keep his eyes clear of the water welling in them from the blow, Shimoda tilted his head back and stared wildly at the tall Dane. "Give me the diary! Give it to me, now!" With the whites of his eyes bulging he tried to jockey Peter from one side and then the other. Blood spewed across his lips, chin and throat turning his collar into a red tide. Shimoda fired a lightning-like kick toward Peter and narrowly missed.

Peter stepped back slightly in shock at the realization that Shimoda obviously had martial arts training and Peter had a bit of street brawling as his only back up. Peter was an academic, not a scrapper. Peter stepped back and tucked the book into the back of his trousers. The ultra-rightist had probably been working in Thys' house just to come across something like this. They were a bunch of crazed fanatics.

Shimoda came at him again. The man was possessed and screamed obscenities. He charged Peter who stepped clear and with his long gangly reach, caught him with a left hook across the face. Shimoda went down, but surfaced with the spade and swung wildly. It narrowly missed Peter. Peter retreated and grabbed a small bonsai and hurled it at the approaching madman. It struck his shoulder splattering him with soil but he marched straight ahead, blind with intent. Shimoda's face was completely covered in blood, as was the front of his shirt, and his snorting through the red river cascading from his nose, gave him the look of a rhino. He charged shovel forward at Peter. Peter dodged and pushed the shovel to the left but the corner of the blade caught his stomach and the rusty metal ripped into his stomach with a shallow five-inch long gash. As Shimoda stumbled past Peter with his momentum, Peter struck him on the back of the head with the base of a bonsai. Shimoda crumpled forward and crashed into a pile of bonsai and broken pots.

Peter looked around, panicked. There might be more of Shimoda's gang of idiots around. Those nutcases would love to get their hands on the Emperor's last diary. He had to keep it from them. The best plan, the only plan, was to get away with the diary and contact Thys when he got home. Shimoda was already coming around. Shimoda stumbled to all fours and was raging. '*What a beast – one crazy son of a bitch*', Peter thought. He dashed out the back and around to the front of the house, where his scooter was parked. He reached it and struggled to find the keys. His hands were shaking wildly. He could hardly slip them into his pants pocket. Finally he dug the keys out. He was shaking and so pumped with adrenalin that he struggled to get the key in the ignition. Once it was in he turned. Nothing! '*What!*' He turned again desperately aware that the mad dog could be coming around. He looked down and saw that in his confusion he was turning the wrong way. He went to turn the other way, but was broadsided with the full force of the possessed Shimoda, who had barged out of the front of the house. The scooter tipped over and Shimoda pummeled him with several blows before Peter could kick his leg free from under the scooter. There was a warm feeling running down his calf. He had obviously been cut by a piece of metal on the fallen bike. Peter stumbled backward over his helmet and grabbed it as Shimoda came at him again. With a quick swing he clobbered Shimoda in the side of the head with the helmet. The rhino plummeted to the ground. Peter briefly hoped he hadn't killed him with the smack from the helmet, but there was a sense of 'him or me.' The thought evaporated as quickly as it had come and he ran to the front door of the house. He thought he could hear the shower running upstairs. He wasn't sure; his mind was pounding. He flipped the auto lock on the door and slammed it shut.

Shimoda was moving still, slightly groggy from the blow. He was alive. That was good enough. In Peter's opinion; the man was already a few bricks short of a load. Peter picked up the scooter, started it and sped away just as Shimoda struggled to his feet. Peter could see the red stripe down the front of Shimoda's shirt in the rear mirror. Shimoda staggered forward and then stumbled off down a side alley.

Peter's arms were trembling with excitement. He pulled over near a convenience store a few blocks later and leaned against a cement lamppost for at least five minutes. Several people passed by and gawked at his bloody shirtless state. Shimoda's and his own blood were mixed with bonsai soil to give him a troll-like appearance.

As he regained his breath, his composure returned and

his mind cleared. Strength flowed back into his legs and the adrenalin and panic were replaced with the confidence to actually ride the bike with a degree of safety. He continued home with the diary still firmly lodged in his belt line.

Outside his apartment he parked and hurried in, never thinking anyone would ever follow him. Once inside, the familiar surroundings of his tumbled futon and scattered clothes, welcomed him like a blanket of safety. His physical state was not good and now that he had calmed, he could feel the beating he had taken. Peter needed to clean himself up. He had time now as the idiot Shimoda would have no idea where he lived. He hid the diary under his shoe rack and made for the shower.

THE STING of the water on his stomach and calf made him shudder with hatred for that possessed fanatic Shimoda. A few quick soapy rubs across the cut on his calf and stomach would be good enough to avoid infection, though it stung like hell. As the water soothed his bruises, he tried to think how he had got into all this mess. His reasoning flowed with the soapsuds into the drain. Did he just have amazingly poor timing? They had tipped over his bike and then hammered him with their sticks. To top it off these ultra morons, now knew he had a book they wanted and Thys was away. He had to contact Rie. If Shimoda's obsessed desire for the diary was anything to go by, the last diaries of Hirohito were going to cause more than just a little stir. Whatever the diaries contained they would add prestige and credence to whatever cause the possessor advocated. It was like a golden bullet of respect.

There were a lot more conflicting emotions being clois-tered below the impassive Japanese exterior than he real-

ized. He was well aware the ultra right faction were fanatics.
In the West, Peter knew that the view of WWII, the Japanese
army and the Pearl Harbor / Kuomintang-Nanking atroci-
ties, still seethed under a two-faced, deceitful veneer. That
veneer of disdain, even hate, was balanced by the lack of
justifications for the atomic bombs and the need to vindi-
cate, the vaporizing of hundreds of thousands of civilians.
The conscience of millions still didn't have an honest recon-
ciliation. He recalled how Thys had said the bitterness of
Eastern conflicts smouldered for centuries. This had only
been a handful of decades.

Peter stepped out of the shower and into the kitchen
area to dry off – there was never enough room in the ridiculously small unit bath. As he toweled down he patted gently
around his calf and stomach. The thought of just 'wanting to
come and master the culture and language naturally in the country,' flooded his mind. It was such a sensible idea at the
time. He questioned that thinking now. Grabbing the stan-
dard first aid box that came with the apartment, he set
about patching himself up. He was hardly a nurse, but a few
basics would no doubt help. Opening the box he found an
array of creams, most of which he could read and a variety
of bandages. It was actually quite well equipped. The calf
and eyebrow were easy enough to clean and cover, a simple
butterfly bandage closed the split on the eyebrow. The deep
scrape across his stomach however was not a pleasant sight.
He cleaned it, put some cream on a gauze strip, and taped it
to his stomach. The scrape screamed at him and he
clenched his teeth. He hoped it was not too bad. It wasn't
bleeding and with a little bit of air and luck it, would dry
out soon. He packed up the first aid box and considered his
next course of action. The obvious option was to get the
diary to Thys. The old man would know what was best to

do with it. They were, after all, given to Thys for safe-
keeping.

With his wounds patched up he called Thys' number to
speak with Rie. She answered but when she heard his voice,
she hung up. He tried again three more times before the
phone was left off the hook.

He turned his main apartment light off and sat at the
kitchen table under a single ring, fluorescent light. He
cautiously opened the diary and tried to read the complex
script. A wave of guilt washed through his mind. Reading
the private thoughts smacked of a personal invasion.
Though his recognition of Japanese language and characters was at university level, he still struggled with most of
the text. Written in the Emperor's flowing stylized hand it
was a script beyond Peter's capability. It was clearly Hirohito's last diary and there was a long final entry, which was far
too difficult for him to read. What were the last thoughts of
Emperor Showa; responsibility, repugnance, repentance? It
was not Peter's right to really know. Thys had been his
friend and that was why it had been bequeathed to him. He
had to contact Rie.

He got a kitchen knife and pulled the front skirting
board off the base of the stove cabinet. He slipped the book
inside and then used the knife handle to knock it back in
place. It would be safe in there.

The heavy metal door clattered shut behind him and he
made his way toward his scooter. A quick cruise through the
warm summer air would refresh him and he could apologize properly to Rie for his rude stare. Though, in his opinion, he wasn't entirely to blame. She started it and he was a
male, so what was he supposed to do – ignore her body?
He'd get told off for that, too.

As he approached he noticed an unusual number of

vans and small trucks parked along the slope on the way up to the house. There were a dozen men milling around the street. Maybe there was a union meeting in one of the neighboring restaurants. It was odd, but they looked normal enough. He didn't need to be paranoid. Nevertheless he would be quick. He drove straight up to the front door, killed the engine and leaned across to bang on the door.

"Rie!"

"Go away, Jerk!"

"Rie read this and call me in twenty minutes please." He slipped a note through the slot on the sliding door.

"I said, take off, jerk."

Rie crossed from the tatami room where she was watching television and went to the wide, open genkan entrance area. She saw his pathetic little note on the floor. It was probably an apology for being such a creep. How dare he stare at her chest like that? Goddamn pervert. She quickly slipped out of her slippers and stepped down into a pair of wooden sandals. She crossed the entrance and slid the door back to tell him off, but there was no one there. She looked down the street as far as she could, but he wasn't there. She closed the door and stepped intentionally on his apology letter. He could pick it up himself in the morning. She went back to her movie.

It was about ten, when she was going up to her room and passed the genkan entrance, that she noticed the letter was gone. It was not on the floor. She must've forgot to lock the door. She put sandals on and shuffled over to secure all the locks on the outside doors. The house was locked up and she could go upstairs have a beer, some dried squid and watch Sumo Digest on NHK. It was the best possible way of driving him from her thoughts.

6

It had been a terrible night. His back was only just healed enough to sleep on, as long as he didn't move. The jagged graze on his stomach sent searing slivers through him every time he shifted. His calf at least didn't seem too bad. It was a clean little cut and left him with only a dull ache. There wasn't much flesh on his legs anyway so it couldn't be that deep. When he looked in the mirror to shave he found an ugly mess scowling back at him. He called it his face. He wasn't sure there was much point in shaving – he couldn't improve on the mess. It would frighten Rie away. If she didn't find him disgusting before, she certainly would now. His left eyebrow had split where he hit the wall and had sealed into a puffy purple mass. The little butterfly bandage he'd applied to close it was lifted from the skin and now perched on the purple swelling like a tiny seagull on a rock. The eye below the seagull was a green-black and the white of his eye – or where the white should have been, was now an angry crimson. To balance the mess there was a bluish purple bruise all across his right cheek-bone. It made his jaw stiff – lovely. His lip was swollen and

split, there were also three dusty rose welts on his chin –
what a disaster. That bastard Shimoda, he thought, a broken
nose wasn't enough for him.

The drive to Sophia University for his classes was a
numbing and painful affair. Each jar or bounce of the 225cc
scooter rattled through the bruises in his body like a drunk
stumbling in an alley. He circled through the main bike
area. It was packed and the four older men who tried to
maintain a modicum of control over the parking area were a
bit flustered and jabbering amongst themselves. They
waved Peter over to the far end of the lot, where they must
have known there was a space. What a Godsend these
retired businessmen were. They were like supermen; able to
organize a thousand bicycles and scooters in a single gesture
and then repeat it on a daily basis. He pulled up and was
about to put the scooter into the narrow slot they had allo-
cated, when he saw two ultra rightist vans parked near the
main entry to the University. Their manic speakers were
blaring away. He leaned across the fence that enclosed the
bike parking lot and stared at them in disgust. He waited to
see if they were actually around or if they'd just left the vans
there to annoy people. In a few moments a small posse of
three fanatics rounded the van in dark blue pseudo military
dress. They strutted like self-important, obsessed, brainless
puppets. He'd had enough rumbles with those idiots. Peter
chose to skip his class and try to force his way to talk to Rie.
He tenderly slipped his sunglasses on and removed the
scooter from the slot. The old boys, not having seen his
ghoulish face simply waved goodbye and went about
realigning and shifting the bicycles.

WHEN THE DOOR rolled back he was surprised to see Chieko

Rasmussen standing before him in her complete and composed beauty. Judging from the gasp when he removed his glasses she didn't feel the same about him.

"Peter you look awful. Come in."

"Thank you. Thank you so much."

She ushered him through to the reception room. "What happened to your face? I hope it wasn't those idiots again."

"Sort of." Chieko showed him onto a zabutton cushion on the floor before a low table in the tatami reception room.

"Sit, sit. I'll get the first aid kit. Try to relax." She called over her shoulder as she left.

She returned in a moment with the kit and quickly set about his face. She had a small bowl of warm water and bathed his cheekbone first, followed by the removal of the 'seagull' bandage. She worked without the least sign of distaste or disapproval. Peter wondered if she had been a nurse at some point, or if this was another aspect of her Ashikaga grooming. In any event he was more than happy to be tended by such a beautiful, if excessively stern, being.

She tended his face in silence. After a few minutes he couldn't wait any longer and blurted out, "I need to see Rie, is she here?"

"Am I to believe you like her nursing better than mine?"

He thought he detected a mischievous tone. "No, no, but is she alright?"

"She's fine, her eyes were very swollen, she has obviously been crying. Did she do this to you? Wouldn't surprise me. That girl may be pretty, but she has a tiger in her stomach." Chieko studied his face closely for a long time. She pulled and tilted his face as if it were a melon to be examined at a fruit stall, while she assessed the damage around the eye and welt. "You won't stay handsome for long if you continue with this kind of facial massage."

He laughed but winced with pain.

"Where else?"

"My stomach and leg."

"Good God! You fool, what have you been up to?" She pulled at his shirt and he obediently took it off.

"Is Thys sensei here?"

"No, he's on his way to Zushii for a few days study." She gently pulled at the loose bandage that covered the angry graze on his stomach. "Oooh. That is nasty, it must be painful." She bent toward his midsection to get a close look at the glaring graze. "I hope these injuries have nothing to do with Rie?"

"Rie would inflict them if she had the chance. I swear she hates me."

Chieko let out a chuckle. "Is that so?"

"I try to be nice, but we always fight, well not always, but often."

"Did she do this to you with her kendo shinai? She could you know. On unprotected skin the sword leaves a gruesome injury."

"And would, believe me. No, it wasn't her." Peter left off there, he didn't want to involve Chieko in this trouble. If the ultras clashed with her family, who knows what would happen.

"So, you did cause her to cry all night." Peter winced as the tape was whipped off his stomach. The timing of the ripped tape was not lost on him.

"No, well maybe, but not intentionally. Ow!" Chieko had put antiseptic brutally onto the stomach wound. "Ow! Owowow!"

"So many 'ows' for such a small cut."

"You were shocked before," Peter said.

"That was before I knew you upset Rie."

"I didn't try to."

The wave of her hand cut him off. She applied a fresh gauze bandage to the wound. "I don't want to know what you did or said to her. You are patched up, but you need a tetanus shot."

"Yes, the shovel was rusty."

"Shovel?" Chieko asked.

"May I speak to her please?"

"No. She's gone out."

"Kendo?" Chieko said nothing, but there was the slightest tweak at the corner of her mouth. She bowed slightly, obviously she had been instructed by Rie not to inform Peter of anything. "I've found something and need her and Thys sensei to help me. Can I call him?"

"Tonight, yes." Chieko had become very cold, polite, but cold to him. His having caused Rie to cry had upset the older woman. She waited, but offered no further kindness to him. It was time for Peter to leave.

"Thank you. I'll go and try to catch her at the Kendo hall." He bowed to the elegant woman. And got stiffly to his feet. She drifted from her seated position as if levitating. She moved to the shoji and slid the paper door back to the traditional entrance on the other side. He slipped his shoes on and as he turned to thank her again, she raised a hand to stop him.

"Peter. Rie is a very special woman in this modern Japan. She is like a blossom, rich with beauty and culture, but like a blossom the heart of it can be horridly soiled and hurt. Treat her well. I have rarely ever seen her cry over anyone, least of all a man. If you should hurt that heart, I will deal with you."

"I don't want her hurt either. Believe me, I don't." The warning was subtle, but accompanied with the icy Ashikaga

stare. It was definitely not just a warning; it was a threat
from a beautiful and dangerous source.

"Get a tetanus shot. See me tomorrow."

He was on his way to the corner when he saw the same
man that had smacked his back outside the Taiyaki shop
only days before. He was at the foot of Thys' street. Peter
sped off to meet Rie. Thys was away for a few days so Peter
could clean up the garden later.

***

PETER WAITED JUST inside the Kendo hall and watched the
final fifteen minutes of training through the glass window in
the door. No one had noticed him peering through the door
as it was located so far from the activity. Indeed they were so
intent on whacking each other and practicing their thrusts
and parries he could have danced a jig and no one would
have noticed him. Staring through the thick glass he easily
located her amongst all the blue draped figures. Her kiai
scream was more piercing and pointed than the others and
her blows, though just drills, were lightning slashes. There
was a bounty of extra intent behind her movements. Chieko
was right, Rie could easily doctor his face with her bamboo
shinai sword in a matter of seconds. The practice session
came to a close and the sensei brought them to the center.
Peter slipped outside to wait.

Rie appeared with her small Kendo bag, she had left her
armor in the Kendo hall. She carried only her small backpack and shinai sword. The sword was wrapped in purple
cloth and tied with a gold cord. She had slung it across her

shoulder. The cord cut between her breasts and Peter resolved not to even glance there though the temptation from yesterday flushed momentarily through him. It was odd to see her dressed casually again. The kimono-like drapes of the kendo session were gone and she wore a loose batik wrap around skirt and long white shirt. She walked with a contemplative grace and didn't see him waiting around the door. Rie was in a bright mood and waved to a few younger students who raced ahead of her. She had obviously had a good session with the kendo master. Peter came up behind her and took a step in front.

"Hi."

She stared at him without responding. A flush of emotions battered the shoreline of her heart. Why did this happen near him? Could hope and hatred dance together? "What do you want?" She stopped and looked into the sunglasses. "Christ, what happened to your face?" Instinctively she reached for his face and removed his glasses. Her palm held his face. Her touch was like soothing ice. She studied the bruising and fiery blackened eye. There was a calmness that stirred the pool of her heart like a breeze across the surface. The face she had watched sweating and toiling, that lovely face, was hurt. She couldn't bear that.

"I told you last night."

The breeze vanished. "Must've been some other female prize of yours. I was alone last night." Her coldness returned like fingernails on a blackboard. To say her tone was grating was an extreme understatement. The tenderness had evaporated. She thrust his sunglasses back at him.

"My letter in the doorway. I couldn't stay, I'm sure they were crawling around. They still are."

"What're you on about?" Rie seriously doubted her

grandfather's choice of assistant. She crossed the forecourt away from the hall entrance.

"I gave you a letter last night about nine pm."

"Well, you delivered it and obviously came back and picked it up, you coward."

"What? You didn't get it?"

"No. What is wrong with you? I thought you were relatively sane. I even liked you, but you're... you're dangerous."

"Rie, please. Believe me. I didn't go back for the letter. They must've picked it up and now they know. Shit!"

"They? Who are they?"

"The nutcases who keep beating me up." His head jerked up at the rattle of the doors on a dark blue van across the street. Peter jumped on his scooter and started it. "Damn it. They're here, they must've followed me." Four men approached with an arrogant menace in their gait. "Shit! Run to the end of the street and turn right. I'll circle the block and I'll pick you up along there." Rie was confused. "Don't worry it's me they want. Go, go." He pushed her away.

His eyes were panicked and the violence reflected in the red left eye made her think there was a lot going on she didn't know about. Rie glanced at the four men who had crossed the middle of the street and jumped over a low hedge. The scooter revved behind her and whipped away. She ran in the other direction and quickly distanced her self from the men in blue coveralls. They were focused only on Peter. They ran to block his access back onto the street. They moved with arrogance and intent, yet they weren't police. Peter made as if to pass them and they blocked him, he spun away and one tried to pull him from the bike but Peter broke free. The bike swiveled under him but he stayed on. The back tire clipped the man's leg and he lost his hold on Peter's collar. Peter gunned the scooter around and up the steps toward the kendo hall. They ran after him. He spun the scooter at the entrance door and then barreled back down at the men, he struck one with his shoulder and the other three scattered. He tore off in the opposite direction to Rie. The men ran back to their vans and the two vans struggled to turn around in the narrow street. By the time they completed the three point turn on the narrow street, Peter had a good thirty seconds on them.

Peter took his first two rights to circle the block. About two hundred yards down the road he saw Rie's batik and white outfit still running down the street. He beeped his horn and as he skidded to a stop, she nimbly jumped on. He felt her arms wrap around his waist. She squeezed right on the graze. His back shot straight as the pain sliced through his thoughts. Though having her close was nice - the pain he could do without.

He leaned back over his right shoulder to speak to her. "Don't hold my right side. Shimoda slashed me with a shovel. It's a bit of a mess."

"What?" Her head suddenly looked past him and her arm shot out. She didn't finish her sentence as one of the blue vans pulled out into the street in front of them. Though the van was fifty yards away they spotted the scooter. "Peter!" He saw where she was pointing and whipped the scooter around.

Being a 225cc scooter it had more than enough power to pull away from the bulky vans and as long as he stayed on the busy streets he would lose them. The only problem was he would also lose himself.

"Where are we going?"

"I don't know. Help me, I'm lost."

"Well, where do you want to go?" Peter couldn't respond. He was too busy driving and trying to spot the vans. "Turn left up there, by the shoe store, then go right. That's Ameyoko shopping district, we can cruise through the crowds. They'll never be able to drive in there."

He did as she suggested and within twenty meters they were swallowed by a river of tourists and students shopping at the street-side stalls for cheap bargains.

The going was slow but they were completely concealed. He continued for about a hundred yards and saw a small turning on the right. The decrepit alley was about twenty yards deep and led to a small neglected shrine shrouded by the neighboring buildings. He parked and they got off. He hurried back to the alley entrance and searched the teeming street for the ultra nationalists in their blue suits. Even if you didn't know what they wore, you could pick them out because they strutted like wound-up puppets. They couldn't just walk like normal human beings.

She came up behind him. "Who is chasing you?"

"Us."

Rie spun him to face her. "What the hell have you been doing?"

He couldn't see any uniforms. A sense of safety washed over him. She had been right, they would never be able to drive down the flooded street. It had been a good idea. Peter looked down at the lovely tyrant before him. She was angry and there was the slightest of mist on her cheeks, just below her eyes. Those eyes he adored, glared demandingly at him. He wondered if they would ever be sympathetic and wanting or if they were programmed to attack.

"Oi! Idiot! Snap out of it." She shook his arm. "What have you got yourself into?"

"I'll tell you, but let's get something to eat. I haven't had breakfast yet."

"We can leave the bike here. There's a Doutour café just

around the corner, we can get something there." She stopped him. "Put your glasses back on, you look like hell."

"Thanks, don't forget you contributed two slaps to this face."

She looked at him completely detached from his attempt at friendship. "I haven't forgotten what you did." She turned and marched out to the flow of people.

He smiled to himself. At least she didn't slap him again. He was making headway.

THE COFFEE WAS HEAVEN ITSELF. He downed the first cup before she retuned with the muffins.

"Wow, sucked that down. Do you want another?"

"Please. I haven't eaten since lunch yesterday."

"Stupid. I'll be right back." She turned back to the counter and he looked at her bum. She had a lovely body and, when she wanted to, could be so charming, though those moments were rare in his company.

THEY STARED out the front window of the coffee shop at the sea of minnows scrambling along the street in front of them. Peter tucked into the muffins like mad. She watched him and sipped her coffee. He had no idea what was going on inside her.

"After you left to shower —"

"I had to, some pervert was staring at me."

It crossed his mind that he could mention the delightful view, but that would result in another slap, so he thought it better to let the comment rest. "Sorry, I'm a male."

"That's synonymous with pig."

"Please Rie, I don't want to fight with you, for... for two

reasons. Firstly, I need your help and secondly, I really like you. You are fascinating. I'm sorry I make you angry but there it is. I said it." She said nothing, just played at stirring her coffee. Her hands were small and her fingers dainty though he knew the palms were hard and calloused. His admission of his feelings obviously got him nowhere. He thought that might be the case. "While you were upstairs I went to fix the Bonsai that was shifted when we were racing around." She nodded. "The bonsai that Thys looks after for Emperor Showa was twisted."

"Oh my God!" Her face burst with fear. "It wasn't broken was it?"

"No, no." Her body relaxed with a sigh that soothed his thoughts too. "But the base was twisted and there was a secret compartment under the tree. I found a diary in it."

"You took it!"

"I had to."

"You stole it!" He could see she was winding up again.

"No, no. For Christ sake calm down, let me finish." She returned to stirring her coffee. "The diary is Hirohito's last one."

"Oh my God."

"It's worse. Shimodasan came in, saw me and demanded I give it to him. Thys said he's an ultra rightist. I think he said he was a member of the Issuikai group or gang. Shimoda wanted the diary, but it was given to Thys to keep, so I thought it should go to Thys. Shimoda flipped out and we had a fight."

"That's crazy! Issuikai are nuts! They are absolute morons, an embarrassment to everyone. God knows what the diary says. The rightists will use it for propaganda or worse. The Emperor's private thoughts. Wow." She shook her head and tried to think of what to do. "Shimoda. I always thought he was slimy. Why did Grandad employ him? Issuikai, are they the ones—"

Peter cut her off with a wave of his hand. "Shimoda's crazy, look at my face. Plus he tried to rip my guts open with a rusty shovel. The garden is busted up. Hirohito's bonsai is okay, but I have to go back and fix the shelves before Thys sees them."

"Don't worry about that. I'll look after it, a few fallen pots aren't going to upset my Grandfather as much as what would happen if those pigs get their hands on the Emperor's diary."

"It's more than a few broken pots." He sipped his third coffee. "I don't know; everywhere I turn I seem to get a beating from someone in this country. It's only been a month."

"Sorry."

"Not that, I deserved yours. Anyway, I tried to read the diary last night. The script is too difficult, plus I had such a headache."

"Where's it now?"

"At my place. I don't know anywhere really safe and as you now know, we are both in the shit. I wrote everything in that note I left you."

"The note wasn't there, so they must have it."

"Sorry about that."

"That's okay, let's get the diary and then get back home. We'll call Grandad. Did you tell my grandmother?"

"No."

"Just as well. If you think I've got a wild temper, you should see what happens when she flies off the handle— the entire government shakes!"

It was then that the crowd spread and the group of four ultra rightists strutted straight down the middle of the

Ameyoko Street. They walked with such arrogance that the crowds parted like anchovies scurrying from some predator.

He slowly turned to face her. She was watching the pack of blue uniforms recede into the crowd. The skin across her cheek was like nothing he had ever seen. Was it like down, like a cloud, like the curve of a snowdrift below a tree? She transfixed him. She was so close. He longed to reach over and trace the cheeks with his lips. She was looking at him with her fiery eyes.

"What?"

"Nothing, nothing." She smiled at him ever so briefly. The smile was like a thought crossing her lips. What was the thought he wondered?

"We better go, get the scooter and get out of here before those morons return." She stood up and he followed the little woman out of the shop. It was odd to look down at the batik-clad figure with the bamboo sword wrapped in purple on her back. He thought of Kurosawa's film, Seven Samurai. If they'd needed a female role she would have fit the part perfectly.

They slipped through the crowd and found the scooter. There was no one around the small dead end alley. The walls of the alley were a grungy ramshackle assortment of wood, tin and old billboards that betrayed the glitz presented at the front of the shops. The tattered walls showed the true nature of the soot stained buildings.

The ash-grey clapboard shacks were pathetic, rickety structures erected only for the purpose of making money. Like old men, the battered carcasses leaned and toppled onto one another in a drunken disrespect. Along either side of the alley was a collection of piled packing boxes, rubbish and staff bicycles. The five foot high shrine, situated at the end of the alley was nestled amongst the garbage. It looked forlorn and forgotten. While Peter unlocked the helmet Rie crossed to the shrine and read the inscription on the plank that hung like a sad smile to the right of the decaying structure. The shrine itself was the size of a large doll's house and had at one time been a fine work of craftsmanship. The main body of the shrine was a miniature temple building replete with inner rooms, alter and veranda. There was a stone donation box located before it. The wood of the shrine's roof was ornate, but had weathered and split. There were a few rusted hanging baubles and the red and white sashes that hung like little tears from the gables were a sight of despair. Rie suddenly swept away the boxes and debris from the base of the shrine. She quickly dusted it off and gave it a bit of respect. She bowed and shook the tiny bell hanging below the roof. It tinkled lightly, a toy. Peter felt awkward watching her and wasn't sure if he should start the scooter or not. She clapped twice, bowed and prayed for a moment, then suddenly turned as if nothing had occurred and crossed to the scooter. She saw his puzzled look.

"It's a shrine to the baby girls who became the panpan."

"The what? Panpan?"

Rie laughed to herself. It was an odd, sneering laugh. Though she bristled with an overweening sense of pride and honor toward her culture, there lingered a distaste for aspects of her own history that coursed through her like a virus, often ready to erupt through a cutting remark or reflective thought. She turned back and stared into the tiny charcoal colored, mouth-like entrance of the tiny shrine. She spoke as if in a dream world of disillusion, as if she were on a raft floating on a river of disgust. "After the war the Japanese government recruited young women to sexually service the occupation forces. Young women, eighteen, twenty-years-old, forced to give their bodies more than a dozen times a day for the sake of the country. Keep the forces busy to control rape by forcing a selection of their daughters to be unpaid prostitutes for the country. It actually happened, sanctioned by our leaders. Young boys brainwashed with military pride gave their lives, the girls gave their honor and dignity. The leaders of this country, the government, sanctioned it. They are so sick and twisted." She looked at Peter who was too stunned to utter any response. "Thankfully the Americans were soon so riddled with venereal disease in a few months they demanded the Japanese stop the forced prostitution. Then, those dishonoured, broken girls either committed suicide, or dissolved into common whores in red light districts." She glanced back at the tired forlorn shrine. "Young girls full of hope, with young loves who had died in the war. Such a joke our leaders. Bunch of foul scum, and people still wonder why the Yakuza operate so freely here. The only bigger organized crime is the political system itself." She turned suddenly and threw a leg over the scooter. She stared back challenging him to speak. Peter watched as the dark almond pools crystallized from a love to the cold fire he so frequently saw pointed at him. "We better go." He gave her his helmet and got on the scooter.

Peter's mind was swimming with a cacophony of emotions. Was he supposed to be embarrassed for being a man? Embarrassed for being foreign? In any event, whether she thought of him as one of the oppressive forces of testosterone driven ignorance or not, he somehow felt a responsibility. He did, after all, stare at her and desire to be with her. He turned the scooter halfway around and stopped dead.

At the other end of the alley – blocking the only exit, stood the four ultra rightist uniforms. They each had a walking staff in their hands. His mind raced what to do. He felt Rie's body twist. She was reaching for her shinai. He had no doubt she could swath her way through them but this was not an option to test.

"Duck," he yelled.

Peter revved the scooter and tore straight ahead. Five yards later he banked sharply into the rear entrance of the rickety shop on the right. The door burst down and the scooter careened off a small kitchen unit. The scooter plowed forward and he could hear the screams coming from the men in the alley. They were following them through the rear of the shop. He drove the bike hard and shot underneath a rack of sport shirts and crashed into a mountain of running shoes. The shoes piled up between him and Rie. He could feel her tossing them out from between them. The bike skidded and fishtailed over the slippery linoleum as it made its way to the shop entrance. Shirts and racks tipped and scattered. Though his long legs helped balance the scooter he was having difficulty with the added weight of Rie. He wasn't sure how she was managing to stay on. The shop attendants were screaming and he could see crowds panicking just outside the door. A rack fell across the doorway and he was forced to turn back into the small shop. Three of the blue uniforms were approaching from the rear of the shop, struggling through the wreckage. One grabbed Peter's neck. Rie slammed him with a running shoe in the face and spun to strike another. The bike had done a complete circle and he punched the throttle to crash out the front of the shop, over the fallen rack of clothing. The fourth ultra appeared in the front doorway with his walking stick ready to strike. A running shoe whizzed past Peter's ear. It distracted the man at the front momentarily and as they passed he saw Rie drive an Adidas football boot into the man's face, studs first. The force of the straight-armed blow threw them both off balance. The bike fishtailed wildly and he reached back with his left hand and grabbed a handful of shirt to keep her on the bike. There was a thud and a small scream from Rie. The crowds scattered and they made it to the main road. Peter and Rie, who was still being partly held on the scooter by Peter, sped away as the ultras gamely tried to chase them down. He released her shirt and she crumpled against his back and wrapped her arms tight around his waist. She swayed and the bike was difficult to control. He was worried she might pass out and pulled over three hundred yards down the road. The ultras had gone back for their vans.

"Rie are you okay?" She tipped off the bike toward him and he caught the little woman in his arms and leaned her against the front of a parked truck. She had lost a few buttons on her shirt from where he had grabbed her and he closed it for her. Her head was swaying like a doll. She reached for her right shoulder. Her knees weakened and she slipped down the front of the truck to the pavement.

"I need to rest."

"Where does it hurt, what's wrong?"

"He whacked me. Back of the neck." She slumped onto his chest. He released the helmet and gently took it off. She immediately reached for her neck.

"Here let me." Her pulled her hair to one side and saw the dark bruise already beginning to form. He tried to touch it. She pulled away.

"Ow! Christ Peter." Her grogginess was dissolving quickly.

"Let me rub it to disperse it." He rubbed the area just behind and to the top of her shoulder. "Now you'll have a bruise on both sides, bit of symmetry, like me eh?"

"Gently!" She slapped his side, right on the graze.

"Ow!"

"Sorry. We're even."

"Even? I've lost track of the account." She laughed and pulled his hand off her shoulder.

"Help me up. We better get out of here," she said. She pulled him down to her and looked at his face. Her eyes searched his face. It was a face she could trust with anything; her life, her family, even her heart. She was desperate to give the warmth racing inside her a place on his lips. There wasn't a suitable place to kiss him. "You're a beautiful mess." She kissed his right cheek. It was the least damaged. "Thank you for getting us out. You're crazy. You know that?"

He nodded and smiled. If only they could find some time together. "They'll no doubt be coming soon. Let's go get the diary. You okay to ride?"

"Yeah, yeah, fine. That was an insane choice of exit."

He laughed and passed her the helmet. "Well, we made it, although I think one of them is going to have 'Adidas' imprinted on his face. Christ you smacked him!"

"I didn't really, it's because the bike was moving. You better be careful you've seen my punch."

"Whatever, tough girl." He stared at her and remembered her shirt was still half open. "Here," he opened the seat store of the scooter and pulled out a light wind jacket. "Your shirt is ripped." He made a point of looking only at her eyes. She took the jacket and watched him to see if he would dare to let his eyes drift downward. He didn't.

"Thanks." She turned away and slipped it on over the shirt and returned the shinai across her shoulder. She wrapped her arms gently around his stomach. The bike purred away. The vibration flowed through her, it soothed the mixed desires racing through her heart.

***

WITHIN FIVE MINUTES they were pulling up to the back area of Kabukicho, a red light, kinky district located just three blocks from Shinjuku station. From Shinjuku station they would head down toward Harajuku, around the bottom of Yoyogi Park and be at his place in another ten minutes. The light changed and he had to stop. Peter put his right leg down to steady the bike and twisted over his right shoulder to talk to her.

"You okay? Do you want to stop at a hospital or anything?"

"No, I'm fine. Let's just get back."

"There's a hospital close, I've seen it before. It won't take long."

"Bull. They get us both in there it could take hours. Besides it's you who needs the tetanus shot."

"I don't like needles."

She couldn't respond as she got pulled from the side. She grabbed Peter's collar to stay on the scooter. Peter whirled around and struck the man across the face. It was enough to allow her to fight free. The van had pulled up right beside them and they hadn't noticed. Another van was behind them and men were getting out.

"Hang on!" He gunned the scooter and they hit another of the ultra blue uniforms coming toward them straight between the legs. The man crumpled forward in pain and Peter shook him off the handlebar. He couldn't go forward because of the buzzing traffic so he drove across the pedestrian walkway scattering people left and right. He took a small side street into Kabukicho.

"There's three of them after us. They're running like hell. Go faster!"

The street was busy and he couldn't go much faster than the ultras. He was beeping his horn like crazy but there was a lot of attitude from the pedestrians in this area.

They were a hundred yards up from the ultras when the road was virtually blocked by an array of parked scooters. He skidded to a stop and killed the engine.

"Come on, the bike's too slow."

He left the bike among the mass of other bikes and towed her behind him by her hand. They weaved their way through the myriad of scooters. The ultras were closing fast. The tide of scooters was parked outside a huge multi-story pachinko parlor. Rie pulled Peter back and shoved him through the door to the flashing bleeping parlor. There was a bouncer at the door and he moved to stop them. He was not as tall as Peter but was more fleshed out and had a permanent sneer etched on his face that beckoned for a scrap or challenge.

Rie yelled something at the bouncer that Peter didn't understand and the bouncer immediately looked at Peter's face. He waved them upstairs. The noise of a pachinko parlor is of another dimension altogether. The machines, with their millions of tiny clacking steel balls and gaudy flashing lights were a vision from Dante's inferno. Peter loathed the pachinko habit and thought if any one gets time off for good behavior in hell, they're forced to play pachinko. The unlucky victims sit for hours in front of neon signs of pulsing women's breasts and legs teasing them while rock music blares over the 'ching-ching' of the metal balls cascading inside the machines. The players sit motionless, glued like automatons to the glass fronted machines and collect little steel balls by opening and closing a trap door. Surely this was hell.

They raced up the steps to the next floor and saw the ultras make the doorway. The bouncer was doing his best to delay them. Two smaller boys, wannabe bouncers, passed Rie and Peter as they all rushed to the confrontation at the front door. She pulled him along and they rounded the stairs to the third floor and climbed. They looked down over the mezzanine and saw the bouncers, who were actually more about show than muscle, were getting their pompadours pushed in and the sneers rearranged on their faces. It would only be a matter of seconds before the ultras would be on the steps.

They ran through the rows of machines each with a dazed occupant staring vacantly forward. At the rear of the third floor another bouncer stood guard in front of the office where exchanges were made. In the old days you could only collect the tiny balls to earn small trinkets or chocolate bars. However now it was big gambling and the balls were exchanged for serious money. It was no different than the slots in Nevada and the money involved ensured that the bouncer in front of this door was more than capable of crushing anyone's pompadour. Rie scrambled to the right and saw a toilet; the 'Ladies'. She dragged Peter through and to the back of the toilet.

Peter was amazed at how clean and pleasant it was. There were cloth towels and fragrances. It was all very chic, not at all what he expected.

"Come on idiot. Stop gawking around. It's the John!" She moved to the back and stood on the sink.

"What the hell are you doing?"

She looked back at him as if he was dumber than dumb.

"Escaping! I thought it would be a good idea. Did you not see them kick the bouncers asses and there will be more of them coming."

"Fine, fine. I just thought it was a stupid idea to come in here in the first place."

"Oh right and who drove us into a forest of scooters. Like that was bright?"

"My driving saved your ass."

"Saved my ass? You got me into this."

Peter looked down and pursed his lips. "Ok. Got me there, let's go through the window."

She opened the window but couldn't see what was on the other side. "Lift me up." He grabbed her calves and raised her up. "Great it's only about a yard drop to the next roof." She squirmed and kicked, nearly taking him in the face twice before managing to wriggle through the window. "Come on, Pete."

Peter stepped on the sink with one leg and reached up through the open window frame. He grabbed the outside of the windowpane. With a swing he slithered himself up and got half his body through. Rie pulled on his arms when he was still only halfway through.

"Ow, Ow shit. My stomach easy, slowly." But Rie just kept pulling like mad. He got one leg through and stumbled to his feet.

"For a big man you're one hell of a baby."

"Oh yeah? You are a pain in the... in every part of my body."

"Thanks." She smiled at him. He was more of a man than she thought. "Lets go." They ran down the roof to the gable. There was an alley below but it was about a five-yard drop. They looked round for some kind of rope or ladder – there was nothing. "You go first and then catch me."

"What?"

"Catch me stupid. I jump. You catch."

"You're off your head."

"Got another idea?"

Peter realized he was beat. He lowered himself over the edge. As he was over six foot himself plus with his arms stretched it was under a five-foot drop to the ground, so there was no serious damage apart from his nerves. As soon as he hit the ground and rolled backwards, he disturbed a bevy of rats that scuttled around his feet freaking him out. He jumped up in an instant and brushed himself off. He hated rodents.

"Okay, lower yourself down." Rie didn't seem to get the concept and sat on the edge of the roof facing him. "What're you doing? Turn around. Lower yourself. You can't jump." It was too late. She launched herself at him feet first. He lunged forward for her and took one of her feet in the ear, which consequently rode over his shoulder. Her butt landed square on his chest as she curled up pulling his head forward. Needless to say he hit the floor hard with her on top.

She was fine.

Peter was completely winded and gasped for air. She climbed off him as he continued to gasp. She put her hands under his hips and lifted to try to help get his wind back. He looked ahead and enjoyed the view of her cleavage. Suddenly she looked up and he was able to avert his eyes in time. She still didn't trust him and dropped him hard on the floor.

"You're a crap hero."

"You're a crap gymnast. What were you thinking coming feet first?"

"That a man would catch me."

"A man catch you! Jump like that you need a goddamn trampoline."

"Least I could trust the trampoline not to—"

"Not to what?"

She hesitated for a moment. "Not to crumple. But, tousind tak."

"Ah, amusing." He wasn't impressed with her Danish.

They surveyed their surroundings and saw that there was only one way out. The alleyway appeared to be an inner courtyard and was gloomy, dark and riddled with filth. They moved slowly toward the other end. There were two figures standing there. Rie reached for her shinai and was about to draw it out when she stopped cold. Her body went rigid. Peter, a step behind, also stopped in shock at the sight. Beside the door, the only exit out of the rat-infested courtyard was a man staring straight at them. He was about fifty-five, fat, sweaty and wore a stained shirt. His eyes bulged from their sockets. But that was not the horrific sight. That was below him.

Still dressed in her school uniform a high school girl in pigtails was kneeling in front of him, fondling him and undoing his trousers.

Rie reached for Peter's elbow and pushed him to the door, using Peter as a shield between the pervert with his teenage whore and herself. They slipped through the door and stood holding each other, face to face, on the other side. The only light inside the room was red, the walls had a dull ochre color.

"Holy shit Peter. Where are we?" Rie whispered.

"Kabukicho."

"How did you get us in here?"

"Me?" He hissed between his teeth.

"She was fourteen."

"I'm not going back out that way," Peter said.

"No, no that was totally gross. Where the hell are we?"

"I think we are in a peep show!" he said.

"What! You brought me to a peep show!"

He pulled her close. "Shh! We're in Kabukicho for Christ sake."

"I don't believe this. This is all Japanese mafia, perverts, all yakuza."

"I don't have any idea how this works, but I have heard of some nasty stuff that goes on in this area. There are strippers, live sex, S&M, kiddy porn, human animal shows it's all extreme."

"Enough, I'm gonna be sick."

"We gotta get out of here fast. They're not gonna look kindly on non-payers."

"Here." She took his jacket off and bundled it up and pushed it into his stomach. Her torn shirt was quite open. "You look at my chest and I'll bust you up so bad you'll think Shimoda was your fairy godmother." She turned around and faced away from him. She put his hands on her hips. She undid her shirt all the way and let it part. "Pretend you are kissing my neck. Just keep your head down 'whitey' and we will get out. It's so dark they won't notice. If you ever want to see the light of day you better pretend you are kissing. Pretend right! Eyes closed!"

Rie sauntered forward with Peter shuffling behind. The hall was long and there were numerous chairs each in a cubicle with men peering through a little open window about thirty centimeters square. Most of the men played with themselves. There were moans and screams coming from the multiple sex party on view.

A figure approached them. He was a big man and blocked a lot of light. He slowed and looked closely at Rie.

She put on a show to convince the looming oaf. "Come on big boy, pull him out." She said over her shoulder to Peter. Rie slowed and rubbed herself backwards against Peter.

Peter was paralyzed in shock and desire. His mind raced. This was obviously to get out, but was he supposed to play along or freeze. He could certainly play along but...

"Let's play. Oooh you gotta big boy." She didn't squeeze him, but her hand was in the vicinity and he pretended to bite her shoulder. He pulled her hips tight against him and groaned. He wasn't sure he was biting her shoulder to add realism or to retain control. Peter kept his eye on the feet of the big figure as it slipped past.

Once past the fat man, an ice flowed through her. She hissed at Peter. "Get your goddamn teeth out of my shoulder!"

"Supposed to look real. No kissing. You never said anything about biting." He thought it was funny.

"Soon as we're out of here, you're toast."

There was a door on the left, they took it and came out into a dried biscuit shop. Rie immediately spun around and buttoned her shirt. He held the jacket over her covering her and then helped her put it on. She checked him and he was looking away.

They slipped out of the biscuit shop and saw the scooter parked up the street. Rie strutted up the street like an over coiled spring ready to explode. A skinny young boy of about twenty walked toward them. He had baggy, black trousers and a ridiculous pompadour hairstyle with a dyed red stripe on one side. He was an obvious wannabe yakuza.

Rie stopped him. "Hey, you want to make 10,000 yen in three minutes." The kid just looked at her. He understood her, but part of being tough was to never show interest in anything. "The light blue scooter over there." She pointed to Peter's scooter amongst the morass of other units parked in front of pachinko parlor. "Here are the keys. You start it up and drive it over there, I'll give you the money."

"That's it?" he asked incredulously.

"Yeah, just drive there, don't speak to anyone or do anything, the money is yours."

"Back in three minutes." He took the keys and walked toward the bike.

"Hope he comes back, that's an expensive bike," Peter said. They crossed the street and went down about a hundred and fifty yards to the designated meeting point.

Rie turned and faced Peter. He was tall and handsome but that didn't matter. She reached up and put her arms on his shoulders and brought her left knee up hard, not as hard as she could, but hard, right into his balls. Rie noticed that it was all mushy and soft at the point of contact. He hadn't expected it at all. Peter lurched forward holding his privates. "Don't you ever try to play with my shoulder like that again. I told you not to. You're as bad as those creeps in there. You were staring at my chest. I can't believe you landed me in a place like that."

Peter drifted down like a crunched leaf to the floor. His eyes squinted shut as he tried to force the pain down from his throat. *'God she could be a bitch,'* he thought. He was gasping for air

She watched confused. "It's not that bad." Rie was concerned, had she hit him too hard? She just wanted to make a point. How hard can you hit a man there, she didn't know? "Peter, come on get up, Peter?" He remained crouched. She didn't really want to hurt him, not that much. "Peter? Please, I didn't meant to hurt you."

"My back," he whispered through his clenched teeth, "pound my back."

"What like this?"

"No lower, gotta knock my balls back. Holy shit. Square on."

"Sorry, really, sorry. I didn't want to hurt you. Please be okay. I'm so sorry. I just wanted to make a point." She pounded and rubbed his back trying to make up for the mad moment of anger.

"You did."

The scooter roared up and Rie gave the young punk the money. The punk said a very polite 'thank you' and after surveying the hunched over Peter, decided it was better to slip off. He had his money anyway.

Peter took the bike and slowly raised his leg over. Rie jumped on the back and waited. The scooter was idling and Peter just stood trying to stretch. He jumped up and down trying to drop his balls lower or at least give him the feeling they were back in place. Rie watched confused. Peter then gingerly sat on the seat and pulled away. She tried to rub his back while they drove. He leaned back at a light three streets later. "Just leave my back alone okay." Peter had had enough of her. Love her or not – he'd had enough.

***

THE DRIVE to his apartment was slow and easy. He made no further effort to communicate and she too was lost in thought. She did not hold onto his waist. He pulled the scooter up outside his apartment. His blow to the balls had now dissipated and he got off the scooter with ease. He held out a hand to help her off.

"It's this way."

He turned to go and she stopped him. She moved around in front of him and looked up "Peter I'm sorry. I didn't want to hit you there so hard. I was angry by that place and the uh... look I'm really, really sorry."

"Let it go Rie, there is a far greater issue to worry about than you and I." He left and she followed unhappy at not being able to apologize enough.

His key didn't fit. Well, it fit, it was just that there were no tumblers left to turn. They had been completely drilled out. The metal door swung back easily. Peter looked inside. There was no one there. In fact there was not much of an apartment left either. Obviously the ultras had connections that allowed them to access information quickly and they had located his apartment in no time.

Rie and he both moved cautiously into the apartment. Peter could clearly see that the cupboard baseboard had not been damaged so they hadn't found the diary. His futon was destroyed as was all his bed linen. The cheap sofa he had picked up had also been shredded and the suitcases and cupboards all tipped out onto the floor. The kitchen area was also a complete shambles with rubble strewn everywhere.

"You really need to work on your interior decorating," she said.

"Very funny."

"Is there anything missing?"

"Dunno, it's hard to tell what's here." He looked for a shirt for Rie. There was a favorite one his sister had given him three Christmases before, it had bone handle buttons. He found it under a pile of linen tossed in a corner. "Here

Rie, put this on, that one reveals too much of you." He moved to the kitchen cupboard.

"Thank you. It's a nice shirt."

"Bathroom is behind you, just push the crap out of the way to get in." He heard the door close behind him as she went to change. Peter then knelt on the floor and with a kitchen knife he pried the baseboard off. He took out the diary and slipped it in his small backpack. She was taking quite a while in the bathroom he thought, but then that was women – some of them could do that. He found a clean pair of jeans and a fresh T-shirt and changed. He also picked up a few pairs of under wear and a couple T-shirts. He slipped them all in the backpack. The contents of the kitchen cupboard had been hurled on the floor and he sifted through the debris for a few snacks.

He heard the door open and she came out of the toilet in the new shirt. She had combed her hair and somehow fixed her make up. She stood in front of him holding the bamboo shinai. She was rewrapping it. She was captivating. There is nothing more desirable, he thought, than a woman who has no idea she is desired. It angered him that a woman who constantly abused him could make him want her so much. He felt like Icarus and she was his sun. He shook his head.

"What? You don't like it? It's a bit big, but I like it."

"No, it's not that." He knew it was best not to say too much. "Everything about you amazes me."

"Can I have it?"

"What? Well, yeah sure I guess. If you don't attack me anymore." He thought she didn't find it funny because she lunged at him. The bamboo shinai ripped passed his waist and thudded behind him. He spun and saw the pain rip through the face of the man who had just appeared through the door. The man, wincing in pain, grabbed the backpack

and tried to rip it from Peter's shoulders as he fell backwards. There was a scream and the bamboo lashed down
across the knuckles of the man, never touching Peter. Peter
stumbled forward and Rie pushed him behind her. Two
more ultras stumbled through from the broken patio
window. Three bundled through the front door. They were
trapped and it was five against two in a tiny studio apartment. The group came at them at once. Rie, instead of
waiting for them to get closer, leapt toward them. She struck
two with her first two swings and then thrust one of the men
in the stomach before straightening him with a powerful
upward blow. Peter was grabbed by the two shorter men but
spun one of them off, who then fell backwards striking his
head on the broken patio door. The other nearly had the
backpack off Peter's back before he jolted straight up from a
thrust into his kidneys from Rie's shinai. As she looked up at
Peter she was thundered to the ground with a massive blow
across her back. Peter jumped past her and kicked the man
who hadn't yet straightened up, full in the face, causing the
top of his foot to hurt like hell. Another man grabbed Peter
from behind, but Peter back-pedalled pushing the shorter
man backward and they stumbled through the open bathroom door. The man fell backward crushed into the bath by
the weight of Peter. Peter turned and lifted the blue uniform
half out of his cramped position and struck him across the
face knocking him out. The short man slumped into the
bath. Peter turned into the room and narrowly missed
having his nose clipped from his body as Rie slashed the
other three men into a brutal retreat. The bamboo shinai
rapped off their hides like a whip on rawhide.

    "Come on Rie this way." He pulled her toward the patio.
He literally threw her over the five-foot high fence, then
jumped over himself. They sprinted off down the street.

They took every small alley and street they could, as they wound their way slowly back toward Yoyogi Park. It was now nine and they were both exhausted.

"I have to get home Peter."

"I don't think that is such a good idea. They'll be watching your place."

"I hope Grandma is okay."

"They would have to be totally off their heads to challenge her. We should give her a call. I'll get a hotel room for us." He corrected himself the moment she turned her head. "Two rooms, I mean. Most of my friends live back there in that block so I don't have any other contacts."

Rie leaned forward into the road when she saw a free taxi coming toward her with its vacant light on. She waved it down.

"Do you know anywhere decent. I'll pay for you, you've had enough trouble." They piled into the cab.

"Aoyama san Chome, Ark hills Place, ni-chome, please," Rie said to the driver. "Don't worry I have a friend's place I can use."

"Great. I can find somewhere." His thoughts drifted in the back of the taxi. It was the first safe place they had been in for the past four hours. It wasn't a long trip but she was asleep in a matter of minutes. She tipped to her left and her head fell on his shoulder. She was sound asleep. Peter paid the driver and noticed he was now getting very short of cash. He also knew that his reserves in the bank would not tolerate an additional hotel expense. It was nearing nine-fifteen and he could hang out in bars all night or go to a Capsul Inn. The business hotels with their honeycomb of stacked rooms were okay but were only made for a man of six-foot and Peter was six-foot four. But it was only three thousand yen so a saving of seven thousand to him was worth it. He lifted the sleeping little body from the cab and the door automatically closed. She hadn't quite woken up fully and stood like a sleeping bird on a perch. "Rie. Rie?" Her head wobbled off his shoulder and she supported her own weight. "I need to walk you to your place. Which way?"

"Oh sorry, this way, it's not far. You hungry?"

Now that he thought about it, he was starving. Apart from the muffins, he'd forgotten to eat all day as they had been bashed from one crisis to another. "I'm starving."

"There's a convenience store on the way. How about a few beers and some instant ramen?"

"Can you cook that, I mean you've warned me before."

"That's so not funny." She took his elbow and curled onto him for support.

The APARTMENT WAS SMALL, but unlike his it had a loft above the toilet, which allowed for a small separate sleeping space. It was obviously a girl's pad and had lots of female trinkets, stuffed toys, pictures and knick-knacks. It was so different from his. Mostly perhaps because it was clean. But then at the moment everything was different from his. He would have to sort that out with the police after they passed the book to Thys.

"Why don't you take a shower and I'll call my grandmother?"

"You sure your friend won't mind?"

"Well, as it is, you're smelling the place up, so I think she would prefer it."

"Tousind Tak."

"Yeah, right." Her eyes smiled at him. "I'll also get grandpa's number in Zushii."

The unit bath was tiny for a man of his size but the water

was hot and the idea of washing off the rat scum from the alley was a blessing. He dried off and stepped shirtless from the bathroom.

"Is that supposed to be provocative?" she said pointing at the blood stained drenched bandage still hanging on his stomach.

"No. That's the least of my interests." It came out much harder than he had wished. The truth was it was very high, but he knew when he was put out to pasture. The kick in the balls had finished it for him. "I was hoping to change the bandage on my stomach. Does you friend have a first aid kit I could use?"

"I'm sure, I'll have a look."

"Is Mrs. Rasmussen okay?"

"Yeah. I got grandpa's number he's waiting for your call. Could I take a shower first and then make the ramen? There's a show at ten I'd like to see."

"Of course. I'll call now. Is it okay to use this phone?"

"Yeah, the number is on the coffee table." She stepped past him but stopped when she was level and looked up. She drank in the lengthy of his beaten torso. "Peter, I'll say it once more. I am so sorry I hurt you. A girl has no idea about those."

Her eyes begged an answer but his thoughts were a whirlpool of hopes. A smile crossed his face. Standing so close to her was like sleeping in sunshine. "I should call." He crossed away and heard the distinctive click of the bathroom lock. When he was in there, he hadn't even noticed there was one, not that he would have used it.

THYS RASMUSSEN HAD SETTLED in front of the television and was waiting for the sumo report to start when the phone rang. It jarred him from his sleepy state. He'd had a rewarding day at the seaside and after a long bath he felt completely satiated. He had come to Zushii numerous times, several times as a guest of the Emperor and they had always enjoyed pottering among the sea life. Though he was nowhere near the expert that Hirohito had been, he still enjoyed identifying various forms of jellyfish. Hirohito used to object profusely to the term 'kurage', which was the common Japanese term for a coelenterate. Yet Hirohito himself would use English terms like coral, jellyfish or anemone.

Because of the cloistered life of the Emperor, Thys never had a proper opportunity to say goodbye to the great man. He was told in a formal letter from the Imperial household, that in one of his majesty's last lucid moments before succumbing to the pain of his last days, he had restated that all three of his venerated aged Bonsai were to be cared for be Thys without fail. The Emperor had demanded they be delivered immediately, before he passed away.

It was a great gift and was disproportionate to the small role he thought he played in the Emperor's life.

The call came at about nine-forty and it was a welcome young voice on the phone. He had been most concerned when Chieko had mentioned that the young Dane had been beaten up again. Thys was concerned that Peter may have somehow fallen into the wrong crowd. It would've surprised him. Peter had come from a respectable family in Denmark and had proved himself in his Oriental studies. He actually thought Rie took a shine to him as well, but then he knew the dangers of any presumptions on a member of the Ashikaga lineage.

"Thys, it's so good to hear your voice."

"And yours Peter. Is Rie alright?"

"Yes she's fine. She's one hell of a woman."

"Yes and you will take care of her." Peter heard the comment and thought it odd. It was a statement not a request. Thys continued. "What is this I hear about you getting in another fight?"

Thys listened closely as Peter explained the incident in the garden and a brief review of the chase. He didn't think the peep show or the arcade experiences would be beneficial to mention.

"Have you read it?"

"I have to admit I tried, but much of the text is in court Japanese and that is beyond me. Plus it is hand written."

"Hirohito wrote well, very stylized. I still have many of his personal letters. The thoughts of a man in his position, the regrets, the expectations – it could be a most revealing and controversial document. It would also prick up the ears of the CIA, even opportunists like the yakuza, if they could get their hands on it, would look to profit from it. It could be worth millions in dollars or in kudos for whichever obsessed group get their hands on it."

"If it hadn't been for Rie and her Kendo skills we wouldn't even be having this conversation."

"You say it was the Uyouku Dantai, specifically the Issuikai ultra rightist group, that were chasing you?"

"We think so. It was Shimoda's group, but we honestly didn't have much time to ask questions. My apartment is trashed and I've no idea how they found out where I live."

"The Uyouku groups have got people everywhere; government, police, the Defence forces and they can put a lot of pressure on people. They're a bunch of crazed fanatics. You must be careful. Rie was with you? So they know she is involved?"

"Yes, sorry."

"Nothing can be done about it now. Is the diary safe?"

"Yes."

"And you are too, both of you."

"Yes."

"It's not a time to be rash. It will only cause more suspicion and hysteria. I will return tomorrow afternoon. Lay low and checkup on Chieko. Everything will be fine. We can repair the bonsai and garden tomorrow. Goodnight and give my blessings to Rie."

"Of course." Peter hung up the phone and shook his head. It was a good thing Thys didn't ask to kiss Rie goodnight for him. Peter didn't think his balls could take another bashing. He turned to replace the phone and she was right behind him. She was wearing pyjamas and carrying two bowls of ramen. He looked at her a little stunned.

"What? You expect me to wear my clothes to bed?" She asked.

"No, no, I... sorry, I should know better than to look at you. Guess I'm a slow learner." There was a problem with the pyjama top and he realized she had wrapped them and tucked them into the trousers. The buttons must have been missing. In any event it helped give her more shape. He tore his eyes away for safety.

"Chill out. Truce okay?" she said with a hint of playfulness in her voice. He'd heard the purr of kindness a couple times in their conversations by the pond and when they went out. It was so different from her usual callous treatment. It was an absolute delight to him.

"Yeah, please."

"Until you screw up again anyway."

"Tak."

"Come on, let's watch sumo digest then I'll patch your stomach. How is your thing?"

"My what?"

"Thingy."

Peter had no idea what she was on about.

"Things?"

"It's in the backpack." He was convinced she was concerned about the diary, but it wasn't really his.

"No stupid. Your lower things. The 'thingies' I tried to break."

"Oh," he thought it amusing that she wouldn't say 'balls.' "Guys refer to them as balls, not 'thingies'. They're fine but thank you for asking. It is nice to know you care about my 'thingies.'"

She slapped him playfully. "Shut up pervert. Come on lets watch the sumo. Daishin better win today."

THE SUMO, snacks and beer, even her first aid handiwork went down with only laughter and chiding. He didn't mind her winning 280 yen on the sumo betting but questioned her 'all in' gaming skills when her friend Daishin had a match. He wondered how someone as petite and fiery as her, had ever become friends with a moving mountain of sweating flesh. He would have to find out tomorrow. It was near midnight before Peter realized he hadn't done anything about finding a place to sleep. He got off the floor where they had been sitting and walked the four steps across the apartment to the kitchen. He set their bowls in the sink. "I better go, you can't get into a Capsul Inn after one a.m."

"Pardon?"

"Capsul Inns, the entrance cut off is one am. It makes too much noise for the businessmen. You have to be checked in by one."

"You don't mean that?"

"No, it's true. I've used them twice."

"No, I mean, I thought you would stay here."

"What with you?"

"Well, no, not with. But you're a student like me and can't be too well off, so I figured; you take the floor and I take the bed."

"Rie, it's nice to offer, but we inevitably end up fighting."

"That's not true, we haven't fought since we… well, since I, kicked you in the, the… 'thingies.'"

"Balls."

"Whatever. We got along fine except when you lost over the sumo betting, but that's because you're a sore loser."

"Ah, that's why. What can I say?"

"Tousind tak?"

Peter laughed at her. "God you're a nightmare." Before, he was captivated by her beauty, now it was the essence and fire of the girl, that made his mind dance with possibilities. He caught himself thinking too much about her and that was a dangerous pastime. "Sure, I'll stay. I'll cook breakfast. You've reached your peak with instant noodles."

She playfully sneered at him, stood up and shook out her hair. She bent over and let if hang forward in a glistening black wave. She took a towel and wrapped the black cascade in a bun. She stood up with the turban in place. She saw he had been watching. He was about to laugh. "You laugh and you're out." She walked past him and touched his arm slightly. She gave it a gentle squeeze. She climbed the ladder to the bed located above the kitchen and bathroom.

He watched her on the ladder. She had to watch the rungs on the ladder and he took the opportunity to admire her body – it was nice, very nice.

She turned at the top and scrambled around in the bedding. "There's a futon and stuff in the oshire," she pointed toward the paper door that concealed the cupboard, "pull it out and set it up yourself."

He turned and moved the coffee table to one side. He opened the oshire cupboard and pulled out the futon and covers. He quickly spread them out on the floor. Peter slipped his trousers off and laid them at the foot of the futon. He lay down and pulled the covers up. He saw her peering from the loft. She had been watching the whole event around the half door that separated the eating and living area. She wasn't embarrassed to have been caught leering at all. In her books it was acceptable for women to assess men, but not the other way around. He pulled the covers tight around him and rolled away from her.

"So, like, who is going to turn the light off?" she asked.

He couldn't believe her. "I don't know where they are."

"By the front door."

"You're closer."

"You're on the right floor, it's dangerous to climb a ladder at night."

Peter groaned. "You're impossible. I'm stabbed, beaten, kicked, jumped on and still have to get out—"

"Movement will stop your muscles getting stiff."

"That's so not true. You're a lazy shit." He scrambled free of the futon and walked to the front door. She was watching him; he knew it. He turned to her just as the light went out and saw her smiling.

"Goodnight," she said.

7

Peter had already slipped out and bought some eggs, bacon and even a pack of microwaveable rice. He'd had one cup of coffee and the kettle was boiling again. They had to get their day underway and see Chieko – he had waited long enough. He climbed the ladder to shake her awake. He leaned from the top rung and gently shook her shoulder. She was obviously a deep sleeper and propped herself up on her arms. She stared vacantly in front of her unable to focus through the intrusive concept of morning. The pyjamas from the night before were indeed missing all their buttons and her chest was completely revealed. Like most young Japanese women she wore her bra and panties to bed under her pyjamas. She had a pale lilac lacy bra with a red ribbon trim. Her breasts were not huge, but filled the B cup and were firm and round. Peter had a long and full analysis before her eyes completely focused and washed the grog of sleep away. She looked down and saw her chest revealed. She whipped the top closed.

"What are you trying to do?" She slapped him, of course,

and he happily took the slap. It wasn't very hard or perhaps there was little intent. Most likely he was becoming numbed to pain.

"Nothing. I haven't touched you."

"You pervert."

"I'm trying to wake you up. You should learn to do your buttons up." He descended the ladder. "Your breakfast is ready."

She was scrabbling around, under the three-foot ceiling of the loft, to get down and attack him. She was not finished with her reprimand. She struggled down and stepped across to the tall Dane. He stood with his tussled blond hair and body full of bruises, but that was not enough to extinguish or even calm her intent. With one hand holding her top closed, she spun him around. He was pouring coffee. "You think you can just gawk at me and walk off?"

He looked up from the steaming cup of coffee and offered it to her. "Well at least I didn't ask you to turn the lights off." She said nothing. He had seen her watching him. "Besides, be realistic I don't think it is the first time a man has seen you in just a bra before." That proved to be the wrong thing to say. She let go another of her slaps only this one she meant.

The coffee spilled and burned his fingers. "Ow Shit!" He put the cup down quickly and ran his hand under the tap. She shifted around just to his left and glared at him.

"Some girls don't sleep around Peter, we're not all conquests and prizes."

"Sorry, I didn't actually mean it like that." He gingerly dried his hand, it was a mild burn and the sting would dissipate in a few hours. "That was wrong, sorry. Look can we start this morning again?"

She had wrapped herself tightly in the pyjamas and

stood petulantly before him. She nodded. He passed her a coffee and she walked past him to the toilet.

"Rie you can't be angry at me. I'm a guy, come on, you've got a very nice, I mean you're well pro—very attractive."

Rie turned at the bathroom door and stared at him. He was actually really caring, she thought, but he still shouldn't have looked. She was glad he said she was attractive, but he shouldn't have looked. "I like my eggs sunny side up."

"Yes Herr commandant." He saluted her as she smiled and went into the bathroom.

***

THEY MET Sammy at the edge of Yoyogi Park. He had cruised over on his scooter. It was only a fifty cc unit and made an outrageous noise for such a pathetic amount of power. Peter introduced Rie right away and he thought he picked up a knowing glance of congratulations from Sammy. It was a male thing, a kind of congratulatory nod. He was impressed with her too.

"Peter, your place is trashed."

"I know. That's why I can't go back."

"You couldn't get in anyway. The police have cordoned it all off. I saw them lifting the floorboards and everything. They say they're looking for drugs."

"That's bullshit."

"I know, but they're really uptight. Especially Lt. Morinaga, he's a right bastard. He gave everyone in the building a grilling at about six this morning. You're not popular in the apartment block anymore."

"Listen Sammy, we can't go back there, but can you pick up my scooter and drive it here then take yours back. We can swap coats."

"Are they going to shoot me?"

"Hell, no. The last thing they want is to have me dead."

"What's this all about?"

"I can't tell you, but I found some papers by accident and now I guess the police want them."

"As well as the ultra rightists. They've been going up and down our street like madmen for the past twenty-four hours. No one can sleep."

"Sammy, I don't have any other options and I need that scooter."

Sammy nodded. He was the sort of friend who would help first and worry about his own hide later. "Hey, if I get to drive a real scooter instead of my piece of shit, I'll do it."

"Please, Sammy, we need your help." Rie said it in such a gentle way that you could literally see Sammy melt. It was so unfair that she had eyes like that. Sammy took Peter's keys. "If you get killed in this whole event, I get to keep your scooter okay?" Peter nodded and slapped his back. Sammy waved and loped the five blocks back to their apartment.

"Is he going to be alright?"

"I have no idea. He's not exactly muscle bound. It's pretty decent of him. We only met a month ago and hardly know each other. But he's a decent guy. He's from Mumbai." She put an arm across his back and turned him toward a low cement perimeter fence. "Sit over there, I'll get a couple tins of coffee from that vending machine."

***

SAMMY SLOWED his pace and tried to assess the police who were milling around the cordoned off area. There were about eight of them in their blue uniforms and helmets. It was completely over the top Sammy thought. He knew Peter and thought he was extremely honest. The police were just being fanatical because a foreigner was involved. The policemen were more concerned with rummaging through the surrounding gardens and interior of Pete's apartment to notice Sammy as he slipped into the parking area. He quietly rolled the scooter backwards and out onto the street. Looking as inconspicuous as possible, he calmly pushed it about fifty meters down the street before starting it. Unlike his scooter, Peter's didn't need too much gas and when he over revved it the police saw him and ran for him. He gunned the scooter and was shocked at the power difference between his 50cc and the 225cc. His hands almost slipped from the handlebars. It was going to be a fun ride to Yoyogi even if it was only five blocks. He took a roundabout route to try to lose the police and enjoy the ride. Sammy arrived back with Rie and Peter in about seven minutes.

The screaming of sirens could be heard as they quickly swapped scooters.

"That's one powerful scooter."

"Thanks so much Sammy. Too bad you brought them with you."

Sammy shook his head. "Peter, you have seriously pissed some people off."

"Yeah, no shit. You go that way we'll head through the park. Thanks again." Rie and Peter headed off between the barriers and into the actual park, while Sammy putted off down a narrow side street. He would soon lose the police.

By the time the police got through the cement barricades and into the park, Peter and Rie would hopefully be out the other side. Peter only hoped they could get out before the police at the other access point were alerted. Tourists scattered as they tore down the fine gravel path past the Meiji Jingu temple entrance and toward Harajuku. Peter twisted the scooter through the barricades at the exit. Three police officers left their little Koban police box, pointed in his direction with their batons and barked shrill commands at him. Their eyes puffed with self-importance from beneath their little caps. The three officers sprinted wildly towards them; they'd been radioed by the others. The police were unusually zealous Peter thought. Three patrol cars could be seen coming down the slope of Omotesando Avenue toward them. He sped off toward Shibuya and thought he could get to Chieko's by looping around near the children's castle and down toward Sophia University.

Rie was a surprisingly good passenger and helped him handle the bike as they weaved through traffic. On three occasions the police had radioed ahead and policemen left their Koban pillboxes to try to block them on foot. One almost ripped Rie clean off the bike and caused Peter to clip the rear of a car that was waiting in traffic. Thankfully the driver got out and released a tirade at the receding Peter. He created such an issue he ended up blocking the police who were pursuing by bike and on foot.

It looked as if they would lose the police completely near Ginza, when Peter himself got lost. The Ginza, Tokyo's most expensive shopping district, was not an area he knew at all and when they were diverted by two rightist vans toward Tsukiji, he panicked. He tried speaking to Rie, but with all the manic driving he couldn't make sense of

anything she said. They drew closer to Tsukiji. He feared
that entering Tsukiji would prove to be a dead end.

Tsukiji, the world's largest daily fish market was not the
place he needed to go. It was an absolute warren of stalls,
alleys, trucks and of course, fish. Peter had come down in
the first week he'd arrived as a way to explore the city. He'd
arrived at five in the morning and the buying and selling
was already at a fevered pitch. He remembered the massive
two hundred kilo frozen tunas being slithered over the
floors along with fresh tubs of live lobster, crab and octopus.
It was mayhem. By this time of day, late morning, he was
sure most of the deliveries would be finished and it would
be just a massive clean up operation.

Three small, nippy K-trucks buzzed toward him and he
wasn't sure if any kind of road traffic rules applied in the
cavernous place. He drove straight and split them. He heard
the drivers cursing. They could add their name to the list of
people who were pissed off at him. He took a left for no
particular reason. Only fifty yards ahead three men were
skidding a huge frozen tuna each toward the opposite side
of the market. Each tuna's head was impaled on a long pole
and Peter braked to avoid the pole but the floors were icy
and wet from the thousands of tons of fresh and frozen fish.
He skidded right and lost the scooter from under them. He
kicked the bike clear and it slid ahead toward the workers
who abandoned their hooked poles and leapt to safety. The
scooter slammed into the frozen nose of one of the tunas.
Peter picked up Rie and dashed toward the scooter as it
idled on its side. The scooter was about the same size as the
frozen tuna. Police were screaming and running towards
them. Peter looked at the six uniforms racing toward them
with their batons waving. The police had the amazing
ability to blow their whistles and scream while running at

full tilt. They struggled to get on the scooter. Rie leapt on and he was running beside it trying to get his long legs over when he was knocked off the bike. A single officer had appeared from the side, well ahead of the others, and tackled him. Peter struggled up first, grabbed the officer and kneed him in the chest. He turned to Rie and threw the backpack with the diary to her. "Keep going hide it somewhere and meet Thys." Peter turned and ran back to the party of six officers who were approaching.

Rie slipped the bag on her back and pulled the pole from the gaping mouth of the frozen fish. The police were trying to hold Peter. His gangly body was proving difficult especially on the slippery surface. Instead of leaving, Rie abandoned the scooter and followed Peter with the long tuna pole in her hand. Rie spun and with full force slammed the heavy wooden pole across the back of one officer. He crumpled to the floor in pain. Another quick jab to the stomach and another officer was winded. Half a dozen uniforms appeared around the corner along with three squad cars and a blue van. She had seen the van before at the Kendo hall. Where did they all come from?

"Go, go, go. Get it out of here!" Peter yelled and then ran further away from her and the scooter. She saw him clothesline two officers into a pile of pallets. The approaching officers and squad cars went straight for Peter. Peter struggled with the group until he got whacked down in the knees by a billy club. Rie ran for the scooter and tipped it up. It was much heavier than she had thought. She pressed the electric start and the engine fired up. She struggled with the weight and twisted the hand throttle as she raised the scooter upright. The rear tire spun and the scooter came up under her. She jumped on and cranked the throttle. The scooter accelerated immediately. It was powerful and

whipped her back. She was going much too fast for the slippery floor and flew out the other side of the market. She left
the fish area and entered the fresh cut flower section where
a plethora of pallets were scattered around the yard. She
weaved in and out of them before arriving at a perimeter
gate on the far side. It was a narrow chain-link gate for
workers only. She ducked down and drove straight at it. The
impact of the front tire whiplashed the gate to the right and
she was through.

Six blocks later, she was in the heart of Ginza. She drove
toward Tokyo station and parked near the North exit. The
Police were nowhere in sight. They had obviously not made
it through the flower market. She killed the engine and in a
few quick paces was consumed by the throng that flowed
into the station. Just through the entrance she knew of a
block of lockers she'd often used. She found a vacant locker
and placed the diary inside. She paid the four hundred yen
for twenty-four hours and removed the key. She struggled
trying to think where to hide the key. If they caught her they
would search her bag and pockets. She had no one she
could give it to. The key had a small safety clip on it. She
undid the middle button on the shirt she had borrowed
from Peter, and safety pinned it between the cups of her bra.
No police officer or right wing idiot would dare check there.

***

THE SMELL of fish was never a fragrance he particularly
cared for, but it was something he and the two officers in the
back of the little sedan would have to enjoy for the next few

minutes on their way to the police station. They had scuffled around on the slimy scaly cement floor and covered themselves in a film of putrid fish muck. The reek inside the squad car grew, it was a longer ride than Peter had expected. Peter hoped that because he was a foreigner, they had to take him to some central station. After another five minutes they pulled into a parking bay and he was dragged from the car. He didn't see any other police cars in the small parkade but that didn't surprise him. Most Japanese city police were on foot or bicycle and appeared to exist in their little koban police boxes. He was taken down a narrow hall. The dingy hall wasn't even wide enough for the officers to walk on either side of him and as a result they kept tripping over one another. A green nondescript door opened in front of him and he was tossed in. There was a table and two chairs otherwise the tiny room was bare. Peter closed his eyes and thought about Rie. He hoped she got out all right. It was a powerful bike and she had to be careful on it. Peter didn't even know if she had a license. The floor beneath him was cold and he moved to one of the chairs. He straightened his knee, the one struck by the billy club, and it yelled an obscenity at him. The club had taken him just below the cap on the outside of the left leg. Thankfully the cap wouldn't be broken, but the blow had bruised the bone. He lifted up his trouser leg. It was the same leg he had cut on the bike when Shimoda tackled him. The welt above the cut was already a dark red and his entire calf felt thick and throbbed.

He waited but no one came. Peter assumed they must've been off trying to catch Rie. They had rifled through his clothing in search of the book even before they put him in the squad car. He of course was saying nothing at all. He just responded stupidly in English or Danish and hoped the 'baka gaijin' or dumb foreigner routine, would work.

***

THERE WAS a knock and Chieko rose from the low table. She had been trying to concentrate on the ikebana, but her heart was not calm enough to produce a centered work. Her worries for Rie and Peter filled her mind. Though she hardly knew the boy she believed he was trustworthy and honorable. Chieko was an accurate, if somewhat immediate, judge of character. Chieko had liked Peter right away, even though he was a little thin chested. He was polite and hard working. He also had a respect for the culture of Japan and wasn't interested in the bastardized adoptions the Japanese youth were so intent on submerging themselves in. Chieko also saw the spark in Rie's eyes that told her there was a fire that smoldered somewhere between hate and love for Peter. As for Peter's affections it was easy to read him. He was smitten completely by her lovely granddaughter and was incapable of hiding it. In that he was sweetly pathetic. It was a weakness of character but one she could accept.

She had not reached the door before it was thrown open by six blue clad ultra rightists.

"What do you want?" Chieko refused to budge from the doorway. "How dare you come in here?"

"Shut up woman," the first man barked.

"Do you know who you're speaking to? I'll have you thrown in jail." She crossed the room and reached for the phone. Chieko knew exactly who the intruders were and that there was no point in calling the police. Half the police force were sympathizers, so it would be a total waste of time.

She was going to call the Minami sumo stable. The phone
was snatched from her hand and hung up. She swung at the
man and he caught the blow before it landed, but he did not
anticipate the thumb of the other hand as it thrust to his
throat and he stumbled backward. Still clad in her kimono
she swung again and pushed him backward. He fell onto the
low table and screamed in pain. He rolled to one side and
revealed the cause of the pain was the kenzan, a multi-spike
ikebana support. It was about three inches in diameter and
had more than fifty half-inch long spikes that were
imbedded in his shoulder from the fall. Chieko was spun by
another man and thrown to the floor. The man who loomed
over her was not huge, but was far too powerful a match for
her. She knew him and had seen him at numerous press
events. His presence seeped into events like black mold. To
her, he was vermin, a pulsing sweaty blowfish. He was the
kind of pathetic bully who became his own god when
allowed into a uniform.

"Where is it?"

"Lieutenant Morinaga, isn't it?"

"Shut up and answer."

"I am happy to say your presence here has never been
missed." He pulled the older woman from the floor and
shook her violently. At forty Morinaga was a peak specimen
of police training or brutality depending on your point of
view. For Chieko it was brutality.

"I have great respect for your family but you have a book
that does not belong to you." He grabbed Chieko's arms and
shook her. "Where is sensei?"

"I'm surprised you speak of him in such regard. Is that in
your police capacity or as a rightist pig?"

He shook her again. "Answer old woman."

"Charming aren't you?" He threw her to the floor.

"Find it, turn the place upside down."

"Whatever you are looking for isn't here."

"Where's your granddaughter and sensei?"

"My husband is in Zushii on research and Rie is with a friend."

"A friend?" He mimicked her tone. He turned back to her and shook her. "If you have that book I will burn this place down."

"Big words for a man whose days are fast approaching an end."

He sneered back at the old woman. His mobile phone rang and he answered it with a snap. "Yes. Good hold him until I get there, I want to get it out of him." He snapped his phone shut and smiled maliciously at her. "We have the prize now. We'll get the other half soon." He spun away from her and called to the men. "Let's go! Now!"

The pathetic little puppet, who injured himself on the spiked dish, scurried past Chieko and pushed her backward over a small desk causing her to fall. In his pathetic, impotent anger he raced around looking to exert his power and kicked out at a Bonsai located in the 'tokanoma' area of the room. The tokanoma is an area of respect in Japanese homes that features a pine bow and most often a few of the family's revered art objects. In this case it was the bonsai of Emperor Meiji. His foot clipped one side and it toppled slightly to the left. Morinaga jumped back into the room and punched the man in the stomach then beat him repeatedly on the back. "Idiot! Idiot! How dare you damage a piece of art like that! Idiot!" He picked the man up and hurled him through the doorway into the entrance area of the house.

Morinaga swiftly corrected the bonsai making sure it was not damaged. He then looked at Chieko who was still sprawled on the floor. "I apologize for my colleague, he's a fool. I'm sure there is no damage to this fine bonsai." He stood and then resumed his rooster-like stance. "I'll be back and you'll tell me everything I need to know."

"In what capacity will you return, as a policeman or again as a buffoon?"

"Shut up!" He marched out. Chieko surveyed the damage to the first three rooms the men had attacked before being called away by the phone. Drawers tipped out and cupboards had their contents strewn across the floor. There was no real damage and like most of the actions of these buffoons it was all bravado. She picked herself up and straightened her kimono. The corner of her mouth was bleeding slightly. She called the sumo stable they would offer some protection until Thys got home. She needn't involve her family until Thys felt it was necessary. It would be an insult to him if she did.

***

RIE DROVE the scooter up through the back gate of the garden and parked it amongst the broken shelves of bonsai. The area was truly destroyed, Peter and Shimoda must have had an almighty rumble. Fear for her grandmother gripped her stomach and she hurried to the house. She could see the overturned rooms before she was able to see her grandmother. Chieko was just hanging up the phone before beginning the task of straightening the rooms. Rie ran along the veranda and through to the first reception room and hugged Chieko. "Thank god you are alright."

"Riechan. I'm so glad you are here." Her grandmother though slightly disheveled was calm and serene.

"What happened?"

"That idiot Lt. Morinaga was here. The one that is so often on TV. He has been nothing but trouble that man."

"Did he hit you, hurt you?"

"No, no. Nothing serious, just little boys shaking their handkerchiefs. I will have him dealt with."

"But your lip is swollen."

"It's nothing really." She smiled at her granddaughter. "I think one of them will have a sore shoulder. I pushed him onto a kenzan and the spikes went straight into his shoulder."

"Ouch, my God! I'll help you clean up."

"You smell disgusting, like fish. Where've you been? Where's Peter?"

Rie took a slow breath in. "The police have him."

"It's not the police. I think Morinaga went to interrogate him. Morinaga might be a policeman in uniform, but he is a scheming rightist. He's a twisted little cockroach of a man. It's not good for Peter to cross him. Morinaga makes his own laws."

"Oh God, I really don't want Peter hurt. He has already taken such a beating."

"What's going on, Rie?"

"I don't know." She glanced at the floor. A long thin exhalation drained her heart. "You probably don't believe it, but I think I've fallen in love with a gorgeous man I keep beating up."

"No, not that, stupid. That's obvious."

"It is?"

"Yes, dear. Very. What trouble are you two in? Has he had a tetanus shot for that rip in his stomach?"

"No, we were going to but then... it's such a disaster." Rie turned to face the garden so her grandmother would not see her cry.

Chieko held the young woman close from behind. She rested her chin on the shorter girl's shoulder and looked at her stern face as it gazed straight at the garden and struggled for control. Rie was obviously falling in love and that was weakening her usually brittle exterior. "You take a shower, the bath isn't heated yet. Don't worry I've called Minami sumo stable. Daishin himself is coming over to stay. He is forfeiting his match today."

"He mustn't he has a chance for kachikoshi this tournament. He's never got it."

"Daishin has a heart of gold and a body of a mountain, he's not one to argue with. A bit like a young woman I know. Go clean yourself up and then explain the trouble over some tea." She nodded and left the serene older woman. Rie glanced at her grandmother as she straightened the Meiji bonsai. The older woman was completely contained and calm, she was like a deep ocean swell, all-powerful, encompassing — a dangerous tranquility.

***

FIVE OF THEM came through at once and it jarred Peter from his daze. He was dozing and thought they had forgotten him. As long as Rie was clear, he didn't really care what they did to him. She had the diary and would return it to Thys and this whole affair could be over.

"You're stupid," Morinaga started.

"Well, good day to you too," Peter responded in English.

"Don't be a smart ass or I'll kick your ass up between your ears."

"Ah, English. At last I can communicate with someone."

Morinaga changed to Japanese. "Don't be an idiot. We know you speak Japanese well."

The light was bright, but Peter was sure he could recognize two of the faces and maybe a third, lined against the wall. Two of the faces were from the ransacking of his apartment. One was the man who got slammed through the doorway by Rie, the other was the one he threw at the patio door, had struck his head and fallen unconscious. The third man he wasn't sure, he was shielding his face. "Well, sir, if I'm not mistaken your boys haven't been doing too well at what did you say, ' kicking my ass up between my ears.'" He waited for the brooding Morinaga to jump at him, but nothing fired. "Seems your pack of thugs keep getting their asses kicked by me and a little girl with a stick."

Morinaga slammed Peter's head on the table. "Shut up, asshole!"

As his forehead barked back at him in pain, he shook his head clear. Peter was amazed that this was meant to be a police force. Being a smart ass didn't work with the Japanese police. "I want a lawyer and someone from the embassy."

"Where's the book?"

"I don't know what you are talking about. I want to see the consul from the embassy."

"I will ask you again. What did you do with the book?"

"What book? I don't know what you are talking about."

"The diary. You found it at Thys Rasmussen's house."

"You must be mistaken. I didn't find anything there."

Morinaga paced around the room. "You study Japanese

for six years and speak very well, but do you think we will swallow your bullshit?"

"I have no idea what you are going on about." Peter was looking behind him to his right so he didn't see the punch until it was too late.

"Lying bastard."

It clipped the left side of his jaw just as he recognized the white taped nose of the gardener Shimoda. Shimoda was on the end of the punch that rearranged the synapse at the top of Peter's jaw. There was yelling amongst them and then it all went very black.

THE BUCKET of water was cold and refreshed the heavy grog form his mind but at the same time it also woke the fresh injury on his lip. He touched it tenderly. It had the feel of pins and needles. He thought that spittle or blood ran down his chin, he couldn't be certain which. It was the lower left corner of his mouth that was swollen and left him with a face only a grouper fish could love. He wondered how many times he had been punched in the last few days. He sure was going off Japan in a hurry. The tug on his hair whipped his eyes open.

"So what was the book you found?"

"Nothing, ask your friend Shimoda. Is he in your police force too?"

"He's an idiot and knows nothing."

"Then I guess we both are idiots 'cause I know nothing. Seems there's a collection of idiots in this room."

Morinaga changed back to English. "You are playing with fire Peter Sorenson. As a policeman I can do you a lot of harm."

"Oh, come on, now. Whatever your name is. You and I

both know my friend Thys has more clout than your pathetic little group and if you get the Ashikaga family after you they'll kick your asses. Christ knows their grand-daughter has already."

"You are a very arrogant boy who doesn't know what you are into."

"Whatever."

Morinaga paced for a while. Then suddenly stopped and leaned in front of Peter. "I am a good policeman and will let this line of questioning end here." He spat the words in very slow crystal Japanese. "If we cross paths I may not be such a good policeman next time. This is a small country with many people. People go missing all the time." Peter just stared at him. Peter had a distinct feeling that Morinaga regularly interpreted the law to his own benefit. "Don't screw with me!" He said in very clear English. He turned and left the room.

Twenty minutes later Peter was tossed out of a police car in front of Ueno station.

He stood up and struggled to the bicycle stand. He leaned against the mass of twisted frames. They had taken his wallet and all his identification. He had about four hundred yen in coins. At least Rie still had his passport in the backpack. He would have to walk to the Rasmussen's house. His knee ached and his split lip made him drool slightly. The walk was no more than half an hour, but with the beatings his body had taken over the past few days, the walk tortured his body like a marathon. His stomach felt hot and he looked down at the cut just above his belt line from that prick Shimoda's shovel. It was pussy and very red. No doubt slithering around in rat infested alleys and fish guts had not kept it clean. A number of vending machines stood in a line along the road about fifty yards away. He made his way toward them. He thought an iced tea would help reduce the swelling of his lip. He leaned his swollen face against the machine as he waited for it to dispense. The internal tumbling of the can down to the pick up hatch screened the sound of the car behind him. Just as he straightened with the can he was thrown back against the machine.

He stared back into the sun at the black shirt with thin pink leather tie. '*How very seventies*' he thought. The sunglasses were very dark and peered back at his bruised face.

"You Danish boy. You look like shit, eh?" His English had obviously been garnered from B movies. "Maybe no so like too much Japan, eh?"

Peter glanced past him at the black sedan with gold trim. The windows were blacked out and it was obviously the gangsters. The Japanese Yakuza were just the people he needed to meet next. He attracted all the scum today.

"You give book to me. I no have to punch your head to shit ball." He laughed at his own threat and the goons on either side, who held him against the vending machine, sniggered stupidly.

Peter responded in casual Japanese as he was convinced any broad vocabulary would be lost on the ignorant scum behind the glasses. "I don't know what you are talking about. I just spent some time with the police and they let me go because I don't know anything about any goddamn book!"

"Ooh. You speak good Japanese. So I tell you straight. You tell me where the book is or I will kick your head in."

"I don't know where it is."

"Liar." He punched Peter in the stomach and Peter crumpled trying to find some air to suck in. "Where is it?"

"Ask Shimoda the gardener. He had it last."

"Really?"

"I think so. That's why they let me go. He probably wants to make some money."

"If you're lying, I find you and beat shit out of you. This is small city."

"Whatever," he sputtered. The B movie English was almost comical. The two thugs let him slide to the ground and then piled into the black sedan and sped off. Peter reached for the unopened can and held it against his lips. At least he didn't take another smack in the face. He pressed the can through his shirt against his stomach. "God that feels good." He alternated the can between the red pussy snarl on his stomach and the swelling of his lower lip. After five minutes he popped the lid and struggled to his feet. He began the trudge to Thys' place.

***

DAISHIN WAS twenty-two and had been sponsored privately by Thys and Chieko since he was twelve. He had been given a good education and had worked his way slowly through the rankings of the sumo world to where he was now in his third tournament as a top-ranked rikishi wrestler. He was the son of an Ashikaga driver. His parents were both killed by a drunk driver. Daishin was informally adopted by Chieko. He lived at the Minami sumo beya like all the young rikishi and trained everyday. Chieko and Thys regularly went to the beya to meet the Oyakata who trained Daishin. Their financial support and respect toward the beya filtered through to all the rikishi at the stable.

Daishin was not quite as tall as Peter, about six foot one, but had a body weight more than double. Weighing in at four hundred pounds he was a brooding rhino of a man with no neck whatsoever but his fearsome aspect was betrayed by his infectious laugh. He treated Rie as his sister and they had been close friends since childhood. Within twenty minutes of Chieko's phone call he was standing in front of the Rasmussen's house. Clad like all sumo rikishi in a light summer yukata or kimono and sandals, he was impassable, like a scowling God at the doorway.

Rie slid the outside entrance door back and brought him a glass of Oolong cha. She had just freshened up. "Daishin!"

He turned and she was swallowed into his arms. As virtual brother and sister they refused to bother with appropriate formalities. "Riechan," his voice rumbled from inside the cauldron of his stomach. A meaty bear paw held her chin. "You are always so pretty. Why have you not come to the beya to see me or even the basho?"

"I am having some troubles."

"I know, I know. But don't talk to me about that. You must come tomorrow."

"You should not be here you are on the edge of kachikoshi."

"Family is more important than getting a number of wins. What happened to you neck?" The purple welts were clearly visible on either side.

"Oh, like I said some troubles."

"I will kill anyone that hurts you."

"Don't worry this will be over soon and I'll see you at the basho."

"Come on the last day. I might perform the closing ceremony, Yumitori. I have been practicing all the moves with the bow, but when it spins on my neck it hits my stomach and crashes to the floor. I am hopeless."

"You'll get it right don't worry. You're famous! I'll be there. Wow. My brother performs Yumitori in Tokyo!" He was embarrassed and waved a palm the size of a pumpkin at her. He shifted his massive bulk from side to side, unable to look at the pretty little girl who thought of him as a younger brother. "I have to talk to grandmother, but thank you again for coming." She reached up and kissed the mountain's cheek. He blushed. "I missed you so much in America. We'll talk later."

CHIEKO WAS pale and drawn from the story. It was not the story she had anticipated. It would upset Thys.

"They were good friends. Not friends in our sense, after all, he was the Emperor. But there was a mutual respect and I think Hirohito knew that Thys' respect was not out of duty but out of choice." She shook her head again. "You have been very lucky to get this far. The Uyouku groups are fanatics and the Yakuza will know soon and they'll want to make money off it. It's like a curse. Thys needs to return quickly."

"I hope Peter will be all right. He looks a mess."

"Does he know you... what shall I say... are encouraging him?"

"I'm not encouraging him at all." The fact that her voice tightened at the thought made Chieko laugh.

"Oh, no. You disguise it so well."

"What? I'm not encouraging him or anything like that. We've just been through a lot. I've slapped him four times."

"Four! God and he still keeps coming back? He's not in love, he's an idiot." Chieko and Rie both laughed openly at the thought of the ardent Peter. There was a crash in the garden and they both went to the veranda to investigate.

Daishin had the squirming Peter in a bear hug and was trying to march him up to the house. Peter was putting up a strong fight even though he was wrestling against a man the size of a Volkswagen. Rie ran down to them.

"Daishin, no, stop please, no." Daishin released Peter who was gasping slightly. Peter stared at the building clad in the yukata and sandals, who had just released him.

"Christ you're big."

"You speak Japanese." Daishin turned to Rie. "He came in the back, I thought he was a burglar."

"No, he's my friend. Peter this is Daishin, my brother."

"You never said you had a brother."

Daishin waved at the little girl. "We obviously didn't have the same mother. My mother was very small." He erupted with laughter at his own joke. Peter thought it was funny too and tried to laugh through his swollen mouth.

"We adopted each other," Rie said touching the massive forearm. "Peter's okay, Daishin, don't worry."

"He sure looks like hell. Did you do that to him Rie?"

Peter jumped in before she could answer. "Part of it, yeah."

"Not surprised," Daishin said as he returned to the back gate and went back out on guard.

"Not big on words is he?"

"No, but big on heart. Are you okay? Looks like your lip is split and you smell like a fish."

"Well, if you swim with tuna." Peter wanted to ask about her, but realized she wouldn't be interested to know how concerned he was, so he kept it simple. "I'm happy to see you got out okay." He walked stiffly toward the house. "My knee took a bad whack. Is the diary safe?"

"It's in a locker in Tokyo station," she said.

"Does your grandmother know everything?"

"Yes. Here's the key." She undid the middle button of her shirt and to unhook the key from her bra.

"No keep it there. No one would ever go there – wouldn't dare touch it for his life." He walked toward the house. Rie was left to close her shirt. She felt a little insulted. What did he mean? She thought that was unnecessary.

The door slid open and the distilled perfection of old Japan stared impassively at them. "Peter, you're a mess." Chieko immediately left for the first aid kit but was stopped by Rie.

"Gran, I think he should shower first."

"Oh, that'd be great," Peter said. "I think I'll need a doctor for a tetanus shot, my stomach is not pretty."

"Not much of you is," Rie said. Peter didn't take the comment well and looked down on the shorter girl. It was the same look he had when she tried to apologize for the kick between his legs.

Peter pulled his eyes from her with remarkable ease. Though he still desired her, the games and fights were taking toll on his energy. "I don't think I should go to a hospital. Is there any chance—"

"I'll arrange it. You shower," Chieko commanded in her demure manner. "You do smell awful." Peter thought Chieko was much more friendly than when they'd last met, which was strange, unless Rie had left a few of the details out.

RIE WATCHED in silence as the nurse brought over to treat Peter worked on the wound in his stomach. Though he wasn't heavily muscled his body was ripped and there was no extra flesh on his stomach. His pectorals were well sculpted and he had what looked like a solid four pack of abs. The wound was a very bright pink and was hot to touch.

"It is mostly just a severe graze and is too late for stitches. You will have a scar. I have cleaned it and you must change the bandages tomorrow. I'll give you a tetanus shot for the infection. Stand up."

"What about his face?" Rie asked.

"It is mostly just bruising it will go in a few days, the black eyes might take longer. They are pretty good ones. His back is better and the knee is also just bad bruising, there is no ligament damage."

"But his face won't get any better? Nothing to make him better looking?"

"That is so not funny." Peter said as the nurse turned him to face Rie and pushed his head down.

"Loosen your trousers." The nurse commanded. Peter looked at Rie, who reluctantly turned slightly away as he undid his belt, lowered the back of his trousers and the nurse gave him a tetanus jab. "There we are. My first injection into a nice firm Danish bum." She slapped it hard and rubbed. "You're done."

He straightened and just caught an exchange of glances between the young nurse and Rie. "What?" Rie protested.

"Thank you nurse," Peter said as she packed her case.

Chieko entered the room. "I made some onigiri cakes for you to take with you. Thys should arrive at the station at 3:15 p.m. He asked to meet you in front of Asakusa Temple entrance near the main red Torii gate."

"Thank you Mrs. Rasmussen you've been very kind. I have created nothing but trouble, and haven't even cleaned up Thys' garden yet."

"It will give him something to do when he gets back. You two get on your way. Look after her, Peter."

"Look after me? It's him that keeps getting beat up." Rie hated anyone suggesting there was ever a weakness in her.

Chieko moved close to Rie and whispered to her as Peter struggled with his shoes. "Your kendo shinai is made of bamboo. Bamboo bends in strong wind when other brittle trees break. Think on it, he's a good man." Rie was surprised at the forwardness of her grandmother's thoughts and the fact that she had also begun to see Peter differently.

Daishin stood imperiously at the taxi door that had come for them. Peter watched Rie stroke the big man's hand. They were obviously very close. He would have to ask Daishin about Rie some time.

Daishin called through the taxi window. "Peter, don't let her do your make up any more. It looks like crap!" He actually used the English word 'crap' and that seemed to give him a real chuckle. Rie stuck her tongue out at him.

Peter had agreed with her idea to go to Tokyo station, take a train one stop and then return immediately by dashing across the platform to the train on the other side. It would make sure there was no one following them. Then they could drift around Tokyo station until they felt safe enough to approach the locker.

***

HE PAID no attention to her when she undid her shirt to remove the key to the locker. She had hoped he may have been more talkative, but in truth he said very little the entire journey to the station. He was quite morose and had lost the puppy-dog glow in his eyes for her. Had she been too icy to him? She passed him the backpack and he unzipped it and glanced through. He took out his passport and slipped it into a pocket.

"Why'd you take that out? Thinking of running off in the middle of this?"

"Thanks for your concern. No just in case we have to ditch the bag."

"Oh right. I wasn't suggesting—"

"It's okay." His glance was dismissive. "Let's get some copies." He walked into the metro area. He was all business. She hurried along beside him. His longer legs were making her run.

"Why are you in such a hurry?"

He looked at her as if she had said something other-worldly. "What? Sorry I was miles away."

"In Denmark?"

"Yes, actually."

"Do you miss it? I mean it's only been a month."

"Pardon? Miss who?"

"Peter, did you get one too many hits on the head?"

"No, no. Just thinking of Daishin, your friend. I'm missing a birthday back in Denmark. I said I would get her a gift and never did. That's really shitty."

"Her?" A stinging thought crossed her mind. '*Maybe he has a girlfriend back home.*'

"Yeah, she'll be twenty-one. Her, I miss. Some of the other things back home, not so much, but her, I do. Her and I are like you and Daishin, well sort of."

"She pretty?" Rie was fast seeing any chance of an opportunity with Peter fade into the distance. She had spent so long being bitchy to him. He had given up before he found out there was any interest.

"Yeah, very. Different body type to Daishin. She's tall too, six foot. She works as a model to pay her way through university. She's into biology." He stopped and pointed toward a storefront. "Here. We can get some copies in here and then go to Asakusa. For safety I don't think that Thys should be landed with the whole book at the moment. We'll copy some random pages so he can verify them."

"Sure." Her friends at the jazz bar had joked she would only ever fall in love with an elephant because it was the only thing with a thick enough skin that she couldn't drive away. It was a joke amongst them. It wasn't fair. She just didn't want a weak man, whose only focus was between his knees. Were they that hard to find? Maybe she'd found one in Peter, but had blown it. Her shoulder was shaking.

Peter shook her and looked down at the dreamy-eyed girl. "Hello. Rie?" She nodded and smiled at him. He squeezed her shoulder, a bit like Daishin did. It was a bit too brotherly, she would've preferred a different tenderness. Her smile seemed to satisfy him and he carried on into the stationary shop. "Then we can get it all to him when he has confirmed it's actually Hirohito's."

***

IT WAS a long and very tedious ride back from Zushii. With his trip cut a day and a half short it had not been worth going. It was of course good to see Tanabesan, the owner of the pension hotel where he stayed, but the phone calls and concern in Chieko's voice had spoiled the whole trip. He wasn't that young and didn't know how many more trips he would make. But then the last thoughts of Emperor Hirohito, or Showa as he was now called, would be of great interest to too many parties. The Emperor, his one time friend, had obviously left the book concealed with him so that he might decide what to do with it. At this point he had no idea apart from keeping it in sensible hands.

There had only ever been one occasion when the Emperor had grown reflective in his company. They had taken the Crown Prince with them, which had pleased Thys. The prince was a warm and natural individual, who never bore the great weight that the somber Hirohito did. They were at the seaside near Iwakuni and the three men, closely watched by minders, were pottering along the shore when the Prince commented that there was an enormous number of empty crab shell carcasses on the beach. The emperor had picked one up and examined the blanched nearly complete shell. 'They are so like us' he said. 'Both past and present. After our life force is stripped away, we are washed and cleansed, then become empty vessels filled with drifting flotsam, never knowing who we once were or what we will become. Surely that is a living death more painful than death itself'.

It was said in such an offhand manner as if commenting on the quality of a shoeshine or the flavor of tea. It had been percolating in his mind for many months, even years. Both the Crown Prince and I stopped in our tracks and looked at the Emperor as he continued, fascinated with the shoreline's bounty. Neither the Prince nor I ever mentioned it to each other, though it was clear the Emperor was a troubled soul and toiled over many such thoughts.

***

ASAKUSA WAS TEEMING, as always, with a bounty of shoppers and tourists. It was one of the great temples of Tokyo and though badly damaged during the fire bombings of Tokyo, it had been rebuilt to reflect the grandeur of it s long history.

The older man approached from behind and to their left. He walked awkwardly, the arthritis in his ankles limited his mobility. He carried a small daypack and of course some obligatory souvenirs in a paper bag for Chieko. He deftly slipped his arm through Rie's. "Hello little one." Rie was surprised at the touch, turned and kissed her grandfather's cheek. The old man bowed slightly in greeting to Peter and then shook his hand. "Peter you look like hell."

"That's what everyone keeps telling me." It was a pleasure to both of them to see the venerated old man. Just seeing him cast a shadow of sensibility on the situation.

"Walk with me. I know a good tea shop near here where we can have Kakigori."

"Grandpa is that all you know about Japan, sweets and ice cream?"

"Is there anything else worth knowing in the world?" He laughed at his little joke. "But you two have caused some trouble."

"Lt. Morinaga did most of this to him, along with Shimoda, several police officers and now the Yakuza."

"The Yakuza! Those parasites!" The old man sneered.

"I think Rie is forgetting her own contributions," Peter said casually.

Thys immediately laughed.

"But mine were out of anger, they wanted something

from you, I didn't." Rie's anger was starting to fire again. Thys stepped in front of his cute tyrant of a grandchild.

"Rie, did Chieko say anything to you?"

"Yes, she said…" Rie trailed off when she saw Peter was still close.

"Good." Thys would never want her embarrassed and squeezed her shoulder. "Let's go and see this document."

The teashop had nothing like the 'old world Japan' sophistication of the one Chieko had taken them to. It was plain and simple with a linoleum floor, formica tables and chairs that didn't match. There were no other customers. When they entered a very old woman called out a welcome from the back room. When the hunched figure shuffled into the shop and laid eyes on Thys she became instantly alive, as if she had lost sixty years. She treated him like royalty. They never ordered, the treats just arrived. The bowls were plain, cheap china, but the flavors and all the treats were exquisite. The old woman never intruded on their conversation merely served them with a constant supply of old world sweet delicacies. Rie and Peter sat quietly and enjoyed the kakigori and specialties while Thys read. They were lost in their own worlds. Rie worried about Peter's affections and Peter worried about how the door had closed on him after all the beatings.

Thys folded the document and slipped it into his daypack. He had grown increasingly quiet during his reading. "I think the document may well be valid. There is a reference to Iwakuni, which is a favorite place we often visited. He knew it well. Other false diaries have appeared and caused quite a scandal, but this one sounds like the voice of Hirohito. The calligraphy style, from what I can remember, is very similar. You have the rest safe?"

"Yes. But why does everyone want their hands on it?" Peter asked.

"Well, the 'Uyouku Dantai' the right wing ultra nationalists, want to see the return of Imperial rule and any document they can interpret to their gain is worth having. And if it doesn't support them, then regardless of its historical significance to others they would want it destroyed. I'm surprised the CIA are not involved trying to protect the gloss America put on the whole dog and pony show that was McArthur's dictatorial rule over the occupation forces; as well as cover up the mickey mouse war crimes trial. Lastly the Yakuza are such a bunch of poisonous phlegm, they would sell it to the highest bidder, or just want to possess it to show their power."

"But what does it say that is so important?"

"We'll have to see. It refers to the war and the nation. Maybe McArthur. We will have to see after we verify it."

"So, what next?"

"I'll compare it to the letters I have at home and then I'd like to read the whole diary before deciding what to do with it."

"Fine." Peter was more than happy with that plan. The sooner he was free of the diary the sooner he could get his life back to normal.

"He left it to me for a reason and that reason must be in there somewhere, though I have a pretty good idea already."

"Let's go back to Grandma." Rie said. Thys insisted on paying and as Peter had only about two hundred yen and even then the cost of about a thousand yen was out of his reach. Rie turned back to see Thys pay the old woman. He paid twenty thousand yen! It was outrageous and must have been ten times the required amount. He came outside in a much brighter mood.

"Everything ok?"

"Yes fine," Thys said innocently. Peter had moved toward the street and was trying to flag a taxi.

"Grandpa, you've never taken me there and I saw how much you paid."

"Ah. The Ashikaga suspicious mind." He laughed and put his arm on the little woman's shoulder. "That is where I proposed to Chieko after she slapped me. It was the only time she ever slapped me." He stopped and looked close at Rie. "Once, not four times, once." Rie felt she had been admonished and cast her eyes down. Thys helped her into the taxi. Peter, with his long legs got in the front.

THE TAXI PULLED up the slight slope toward Thys Rasmussen's house. Peter was watching the street for suspicious looking vans or more of the rightist blue uniforms. It was the sunglasses that gave the man away to Peter. He was near the corner bent down buying cigarettes from a vending machine. It was the black shirt Yakuza. As he turned to view the taxi Peter could see the pink tie. They made eye contact and the Yakuza whipped out his mobile phone and ran up the street after them.

"Keep going. Don't stop."

"What? Why?"

"The Yakuza are behind us."

The driver looked in the rearview mirror and mumbled. A blue van was on the side of the road and it looked like everyone had been waiting for their return. They continued past the house and saw Daishin with another young sumo rikishi standing in front of the house.

"To the Minami sumo beya right away." Thys called to the driver.

"I don't want any trouble," the driver said, but his voice was drowned out by the van pulling away from behind. The Ultra Nationalists had their message blaring full volume.

"Just get us there." Thys barked at the confused driver. "It's just past Uchsaiwaicho station. You get us there and you won't have any trouble. If we don't make it, you won't know what has hit you."

"Yes, yes of course." The little driver obviously thought of his own tail before anything else in his world and drove for all he was worth, shifting lanes repeatedly. Though he refused to speed, he did, only just, squeeze through a few lights. The van proved hard to shake and arrived within ten seconds of their taxi. The three of them piled out and ran for the entrance to the practice dojo. Young wrestlers would be still in second training before their evening chores and bathing. Thys burst through with Peter slamming the door behind the three of them. All heads turned to them. It was a huge shock for Peter. He had never seen so much weight assembled with so little clothing and no beach. The shaggy haired wrestlers of varying sizes and ages were all covered in caked on sand-sweat. Another car screeched to a halt outside.

"Carry her on your back Peter. Her feet don't touch the dojo." Thys commanded and Rie climbed aboard. They scampered through the crowd of sweaty pale walruses. On the far side the Oyataka stood on a tatami and welcomed them over.

"Oyatakasan, please forgive this intrusion. I need your help immediately."

"No, no Sensei your presence here is good fortune for us. Daishin is —"

The door burst open and half a dozen ultra nationalists burst through. Their small tight blue uniforms looked ridiculous against the forest of pear shaped, sweating mass before them. The Uyouku Dantai blue uniforms had come prepared and all carried wooden batons.

The rikishi did not like intrusions in their sumo domain and these buffoons were the last they wanted to see. They were happy to allow the respected old man and even Rie to enter as she was appropriately carried across the practice dojo by the beaten up foreigner. The rightists were a much more unpleasant intrusion. The collection of uniforms warily edged to one side of the training hall. They scuttled like feeder fish at the mouth of a shark gingerly trying to pick scraps without being noticed.

"This way Sensei. Who is the foreigner?" They followed the massive retired sumo to the rear of the building.

"My bonsai assistant." Thys wasn't sure why he said it, but it had the desired effect as the big man stopped and faced the tall lanky frame of Peter.

"You okay speak, Japanese?"

"Yes, sir."

"Good. Please put that beautiful girl down and learn to fight, your face is a mess. No man should look like that."

"Sorry. I ah… "

"Don't say you are sorry, do better next time."

"Yes, sir."

"Oyatakasan." Thys interrupted. "Peter has important papers from Emperor Showa, which belong to me and those idiots want them. The police are after us too."

"Who? That asshole Morinaga?"

"You know him?" Rie asked. The big man nodded as he crossed past her and Peter. He stopped in front of Peter. The sumo's face and neck, if there was one, was so wide he lost sight of Thys completely. He glared at Peter.

"Morinaga do this to you?"

"And some others," Peter said sheepishly.

The sumo grinned at him and nimbly hopped back three steps toward the fight that could be heard through the door. An enormous bellow shattered the fight. "Crush these scum! They have insulted Daishin's family!" There was a huge bloody roar behind him as he returned with an enormous smile on his face. "The boys will just love that. Come this way." They followed the big man to the rear of the building. There was a stunning woman sitting behind the wheel of an expensive Nissan Skyline Turbo. She revved the engine. They piled in. As the stable master spoke to the angel behind the wheel, two Yakuza bosozoku motorbikes with their howling mufflers pulled down the alleyway and gunned their engines. Each bike had a passenger. Peter watched as the big retired sumo waved to Thys, turned and ran straight at the oncoming bikes. The Japanese angel 'a la Shumacher' smoked the tires away. Peter watched the massive man throw himself at both bikes with his arms outstretched. He clotheslined both riders and their pillion passengers off the bikes. Surely he must've dislocated both his shoulders. He could see no more as he was thrown on top of Rie as the supercharged sports car drifted around a corner. Peter had seen this kind of driving on television, but to sit in the back and experience it during rush hour was a fear he had never known; a sense of rush and terror at the same time. Yet the angel, wannabe Shumacher, was completely calm, she even smiled in the rearview mirror.

The driver looked at Thys. "I am sorry sensei, but my husband said to get you home as quickly as I could."

"Don't worry Peter, the Oyakata's wife has always driven like this, even before they gave her a license. Did you get it back?"

"Sort of. Got it and lost it again." They both laughed. "I've stopped asking for it now."

She took the corner at the bottom of the hill at nearly sixty and Peter only saw the parked cars in front of them as they drifted virtually sideways up the hill. They whipped back straight and screeched to a halt. Daishin, who was in front of the house, opened sensei's door and then helped Rie from the back seat. The driver jumped out and put her seat forward for Peter. When he stepped out he thought he had lost sight of her. She wasn't even five foot tall and had an absolutely gorgeous body. *'She was the sumosan's wife? Impossible,'* he thought.

"Come by for a cruise again sometime," she said.

Peter was trying not to fall down, he was so happy to be out of the car. "Yeah, yeah love to."

Daishin called across the cab of the purring car. "Peter you need the toilet? Her driving scares the shit out of most people."

"Funny, Daichan." He smiled back at her nickname for him. 'Chan' for little girl, was anything but a description of the mammoth sumo. With a peel of her tires she was gone and the four of them stood staring at one another all slightly shaken.

Daishin waved at the receding car. "Oyatakasan says she drives like a martini. Stirred and shaken!" He erupted with an immense laugh that shuddered like an earthquake through his frame.

Thys went into the house. Followed by the other three. Chieko was there to greet her husband, which she did in the most formal of manners. Thys lifted her off the floor where she was kneeling. He touched her lip tenderly. It was ever so slightly swollen. She turned away and they followed her.

"Peter because you and Rie still have the diary with you,

it is best if you don't stay. We must keep the documents safe. You have been lucky so far, so you should stay together. I'll examine the copies here."

"I really don't think Rie wants to be around me anymore."

"Why would that be?" She snapped not wanting her wishes expressed by anyone other than herself.

"Well, you are always getting hurt and angry."

"Look at your face. It is you that's always hurt and I'm angry because I have to keep saving your ass!"

"Well, then," Thys interrupted, "I guess you better stay together."

"I'll look after him," Rie slipped in.

"You'll look after me!" Peter wasn't taking her pushy crap anymore.

"Okay you two, let's keep ourselves together," Chieko said calmly as she slipped her arms between theirs to lead them toward the garden. "Can you find somewhere safe for tonight?"

"We're staying at Nakamura's, she's in Thailand."

"That's on Aoyama san Chome isn't it?" Chieko asked.

"Yes, it's safe and has enough room for two," Rie said innocently.

Thys moved to Rie's side. "I'll review this copy to verify it as close as I can and call you tomorrow morning. Then we can decide what is best for the diary. I'll also call the chamberlain and inform him."

"Really? Do we need to go that far?" Peter asked. "It was left to you. Do you want the Imperial household involved?"

"Two reasons Peter. Firstly the Japanese for better or worse are still attached to the Emperor and secondly he was my close friend and it is an Imperial document."

Thys put his arm around Rie and ushered her to the

veranda. "Daishin will stay here with two other rikishi all night, so we will be fine. You two should go and get some rest. It will be a big day tomorrow, whatever we decide."

"Your bike is in the back yard Peter, let's go," Rie said.

Peter stood up as Rie made her way down the veranda. He stopped in front of Thys. "I destroyed your Bonsai shelves when Shimoda and I had a fight. I am terribly sorry. I will fix them tomorrow and Monday I promise."

Chieko stepped forward. "Not to worry Peter, you're busy. But thank you."

Peter wasn't sure if it was a kindness or a rebuff, in any case he had to leave as Rie was tugging at his sleeve.

At the foot of the garden he found why his services were not needed. Three young sumo trainees, no more than fourteen years old, but already outweighing Peter, had just finished sweeping the bonsai area. Everything had been put back exactly as it was. He turned back to the veranda. Thys had gone in, but Chieko was there watching them leave. She bowed farewell. It reminded Peter of the takenoko bamboo fountain in the teashop when he first met Rie. When it filled with water and tipped ever so gracefully forward – it was the same serenity of movement. He realized that with his six years of education in Japanese language, he actually knew nothing. In one bow it had been brought home to him. He knew nothing.

He backed the scooter out. Rie jumped on the back and they slipped away down the back street.

It was eight by the time they got through the traffic and arrived at the apartment with their take-away sushi. Thankful to be safe at last they both collapsed on the floor. He soon dropped off to sleep and she went into the tiny unit bath to bathe.

When she came out half an hour later, he had woken up

and prepared all the sushi on a table with some beer. She wore only a towel around her and he stared in wonder at what may lay beneath the white cloth. She caught him staring and he could see her eyes start to glow.

"What, what?" he protested. "I was just noticing that you had only a, a towel on and still, you, you could make it look nice." She accepted his stuttered excuse. "Hurry up and get changed so we can watch sumo digest."

She drew the shoji door closed but there was only one, not two, like there normally would be. She couldn't block off the whole kitchen area where she planned on getting changed. The bathroom was too steamy. She leaned through the half open doorway. "There is only one shoji so I can't close it. You peek and I will hurt you, seriously." Peter just waved and she receded to the far corner of the room.

Peter being a man had to at least glance toward the door. He would in no way consider invading her privacy. However as he moved his head back toward the TV set, his eyes caught movement reflected on the glass microwave door. He watched as she clipped her bra closed and pulled the pyjama shirt around her tying it at the base. Though the figure was very fuzzed, she had a gorgeous body. She seemed to be looking back at him through the reflection and he dared not move his head. He wasn't sure if she had spotted him, the view was very hazy at best anyway. Suddenly she moved forward and slid the door open to the other side of the tracks. He closed his eyes and pretended to be asleep. She watched him for several seconds then moved beside him and gently shook him awake.

"Come on let's eat. You can sleep later." The familiar clacking of the cedar blocks heralded the start of the program. Sumo Digest was the wrap up of the daily bouts in a very condensed form, but it still carried the fun of the competition. Daishin had somehow returned for his bout and then made it back to Thys' place before they had arrived that afternoon. He must have received some kind of permission from the tournament itself. Daishin hadn't even mentioned that he had won. Rie knew everything about sumo from the throws, to the ceremonies, to the taboos and traditions. She even said she wouldn't mind being a sumo's wife as wrestlers were known to be wealthy, cultured and usually had very kind hearts. She also said they didn't need protecting and gave him a playful jab in the ribs. Her fingers got wet though. She looked down. His shirt was soaked through, the bandage had been leaking.

"Get your shirt off."

"Wow, you're subtle, no foreplay."

"Very funny. Come on Pete, you're bleeding."

"Huh?" He looked down at his right side. Just above the waist was a big red stain. It had been seeping for a few hours, probably because of the bike ride. He unbuttoned his shirt and she helped him take it off.

"I'll wash this and get the first aid kit. I'm sure she has some bandages."

He lay on the floor and she dabbed the wound. He watched her as her long hair fell forward. He couldn't help thinking of her beauty. He was so enthralled by her. He had tried all day to put her out of his mind, but her being rushed at him like an avalanche. It wasn't the view in the microwave door or anywhere else. Her body was desirable, but that wasn't what twisted him inside. It was her eyes and face, her skin, her smile. He closed his eyes blocking her out of his thoughts.

She spoke to him without looking up. "You better not be looking down my top you pervert."

"I'm not. I was looking at your eyes and thinking." He

paused, as a thought crossed his mind, *Why not be honest, he will just get slapped again. It was becoming a habit.* "I was thinking how lucky some big fat sumo will be, if you fall for that kind of man."

"Well, it certainly won't be for a man as skinny as you. Why don't you make your twenty-one year old Danish girlfriend feed you more?"

"What? I don't have a girlfriend. You mean my sister. No, no she's as crappy a cook as you. No, that's not true, no one is as crappy as you."

"Whatever. At least I only have one weak point."

"Oh, right."

She leaned forward and put a finger on his lips. "Come on, truce in here, right?"

With her fingers on his lips, if she'd asked him to go fight the mass of sweating sumos in the stable earlier today, he would have happily gone. The avalanche of wonder was sweeping him again.

"Let's take a peek at the diary," she said.

The next two hours were spent trying to understand the archaic court language used by Hirohito. It was hard going, even for Rie.

When the corner of the book fell on his thigh he opened his eyes. She was sleeping with her face pressed against his bare chest. He could feel her warm slow breath drift across his nipples. Her hair had fallen loose across his belly. He tried to move out from under her but she stirred and looked up at him. He wished she'd never move.

She glanced up keeping her head close to his chest. An impulse raced over her and without a second thought she leaned back down and left a slow hot kiss on his chest. "There that is the only place undamaged on you. I'm going to bed." She stood up and stretched in front of him.

She was so on display and so far away. Did she really have no idea he was crazy about her? She turned and trudged to the ladder and climbed up to the loft.

She called over her shoulder, "you know where the stuff is right." She didn't wait for his answer as she dived into the futon.

8

I t was ten before the call came from Thys. They had expected a response much sooner, but as he was a very particular scientist he would no doubt have taken his time in doing as thorough a study as possible. Rie had been awake for an hour and had washed Peter's bloodied shirt. She had also cleaned the apartment and prepared a simple breakfast for them both. Peter did little more than shower and purchase a newspaper. He couldn't concentrate on reading it. Peter's mind was far too preoccupied with Thys' response and the movements of Rie. She was very relaxed around him.

The phone startled them both. Peter answered it.

"Peter, it seems as near as I can tell, you have the last diary of Emperor Showa."

"Okay, I guess that's good news, but what do we do with it now? He left it with you for good reason."

"I think we should meet as soon as possible. I want to read it and then decide what he would have wanted me to do."

"Fine. I'll bring it, where do you want to meet?"

"I'll meet you for Taiyaki at Ueno. Then you'll know the real flavor of anko paste. About eleven should be good. How is that for you?" Peter never heard Thys on the phone again. Male voices rattled in the background and he could hear Daishin barking out orders. There was lots of screaming from young male voices. Peter thought he heard a wall get knocked down and then Thys yelling at the intruders. There was an unmistakable voice that yelled out. The phone went dead. That voice was the swine Morinaga.

DAISHIN HAD only seconds to prepare as they streamed out of the vans. There were more than twenty of them and he had only two sixteen year olds to hold them off. He kept them out of the house until the second sixteen-year-old went down under a hail of wooden sticks. Daishin backed into the entryway and threw the blue screaming uniforms back on top of each other. Trained mostly in power and technique his only means of defense was to take several blows in order to land a thunderous clout or crush one of the disgusting ants. A blow to the head from a baton made him stumble backwards and through the paper shoji. Thys was still on the phone when Daishin glanced at him before drifting briefly unconscious. Batons rained down on him, but his senses were fading.

Shimoda leapt across and snatched the phone from Thys' hand and hurled it to one side. Morinaga wrapped his hand tightly on the old man's throat and lifted him from his seated position on the floor. He threw Thys toward Daishin. The impact of the body slowly roused Daishin. Morinaga stared at the papers that Thys had been reviewing. The copies of the diary engulfed his intentions in flames. He ran to Thys and pulled him from the floor.

"You foreign bastard. Where is it?"

"It has nothing to do with you, you scum," Thys said.

Morinaga slapped the older man across the face with the back of his hand. Daishin was about to get to his feet when he saw white tabi socks at the top of the steep stairs on the other side of the door. Chieko knelt down and looked at him. She'd caught his eye. She had an old kendo sword in her hand. Daishin knew that it was because of her that Rie had taken up kendo, but surely the grandmother was not intent on putting up a fight. Then again she was an Ashikaga. She nodded to the garden, which he took to be the exit for Thys.

Morinaga moved in on Thys again. He had a wooden staff and pressed it hard against the base of Thys' neck. "Where is it? Does the tall foreign kid have it? The girl?"

If there is one thing a sumo wrestler possesses it is flexibility and that, fueled by insult and anger propelled the two hundred kilogram mass of Daishin to spin on the floor and in one movement slide up and chop Morinaga across the throat with a meaty palm.

"Get out through the garden, sensei!" Shimoda came at Daishin with his staff and the sumo took the blow on his forearm. Two more blows rained down before he was able to tie up Shimoda in his massive arms and hurl him back onto Morinaga. More of the blue uniformed ants scrambled through the door. Chieko standing on the third step slashed down at them as they came through. She took two in the face on her first blow and the third was chopped in the throat. She jumped from the step and faced all three brandishing their staffs toward her. There was a look of fear and anger in their eyes. Could they justify hitting an old woman? They glanced at how she held the kendo practice sword. She held it like an expert. Their nerves wavered. Two of their colleagues lay unconscious on the floor and a third was drowning in his own blood as it streamed from his ruptured throat. If she was an old woman she was playing to kill not just to overcome. Morinaga threw Shimoda off him and went at the bulk of Daishin. Daishin had to take a few blows in order to land one, but Daishin's blow usually knocked a man flat to the floor. Morinaga was different and went for Daishin's knees. He got Daishin to the ground where he kicked him in the face. Shimoda also landed a blow to Daishin's cheek before being struck unconscious with a blow to the back of the head. Chieko had silenced him with one glancing blow. Morinaga turned to her, but Daishin grabbed his neck and launched him at the crowd of six uniforms swirling like confused bugs in the doorway. Chieko and Daishin backed into the garden. Chieko glanced down to the end of the garden and saw Thys look back to her. She smiled and raised her eyebrows at him. Thys knew she was having the time of her life, he could not pull her from it. Her Ashikaga pride and kendo scream roared forward at the assailants as he slipped out the gate. The eight men came at them. The path in the garden was narrow and Chieko would take on a few before retreating and allowing the charging rhino behind her to drive them back. Though Daishin took numerous blows they could not knock him down and at every chance she would deftly slash blows down upon them. There was an impasse reached. The ultra nationalists had reduced to only four, but that still included Morinaga. Chieko and Daishin were cornered with their backs to the gate.

"He's gone!" Shimoda screamed from his position on the floor. His eye streamed with blood.

"What?"

"Sensei has gone out the back!"

"Shit!" Morinaga was livid and backed up several paces." Around to the back! Search the alley. You others, into the vans. Quickly! I heard him mention Ueno."

The vermin needed no further encouragement to retreat from the bull and the mad old woman. They scurried up and out of the house dragging their dead colleague with them. The blood left an ugly smear across the entrance. A trail of stupidity Chieko thought. Daishin was about to run after them.

"Let them go."

"But sensei could be caught on the street." The big man protested.

"No, he's too clever for that. Wait here a moment." She picked the phone from the floor. It still worked. "We need some other help. I must call my brother he will send some support for Thys. We have used these people before."

Daishin stood a little ashamed at not having been able to protect his stepmother. In the entrance way the two sixteen-year-olds watched sheepishly, their faces bleeding from the blows of the batons. Daishin waved them into the house.

Chieko turned to them. "My God, you've done well. Such brave young men. Come, I will clean you up. Daishin you must go."

"I'll go to Ueno and—"

"No, you will go to the basho. You cannot miss another match."

"Sumo means nothing if—"

"Shut up and do as you are told. You are like my son. You must do as I say. Sensei will be fine. You must do it. There is no further discussion. I will call the beya and ask that they fix your face before you fight. You look like Peter."

"Yes ma'am." The gargantuan's heart was now more battered than his body, he visibly shrank before her.

"Daishin you are an absolute demon. We held twenty of them. We would have been lost without you. If they had caught Thys, they would have bartered for the diary. You stopped that. We are so proud of you. But now do as you are told. Goodbye. You must win for us today." She turned to the two younger boys.

Daishin knew that there was no point in arguing against the edict. He turned and limped from the room.

The battered sumo slowly walked to the base of the hill. He straightened his blood-spattered yukata robes and wiped the blood from his neck, mouth and face. He wasn't sure he would get a taxi or not in his bloodied state. The first taxi to come by recognized him immediately and he was whisked to the Basho. He still had a few hours before he was due at his afternoon bout. He was seven wins and seven losses, today was the last day and the roads even now would be busy near the Kokugikan hall. Sitting in the back of the taxi he wondered how he could possibly fight with Thys sensei in so much difficulty. He would fight for the family.

***

WITH THE CLOSING of the back gate his heart was torn between wanting to stay and protect his love, and the love he had to let her enjoy the battle. As an Ashikaga, she wore her honor and family pride like a badge of fury. Thys could not deny her this moment. It would be an unforgivable blow to her heart to not let her fight. She was the pride of the

Ashikagas for her intense pursuit of the bushido spirit, even
though she was a woman. He could not deny her the pleasure of the challenge. It would be manly, but unloving to try
to protect her. Besides which, with her kendo and the
volcano that was Daishin beside her, it was a very even
contest.

The 'tweet-tweet' of a natto seller's horn made Thys
jump. The snaggle-toothed ninety-year-old came around
once a week and sold the old-fashioned smelly soya bean
treat from his bicycle. The tradition was hundreds of years
older than the rider himself. He wore a simple shirt with
pyramid shaped reed hat, a kind of waraboshi called sugegasa. Thys stopped him.

The old man recognized the well-known sensei and
bowed deeply. The sensei's wife was a very regular
customer.

"I'll give you twenty thousand yen for your bicycle and
bamboo sugegasa hat?"

"What? No, Sensei I'm selling natto."

"I know, I know. Look I need it now. Give me the hat and
bicycle. Here this is all I have now. Come back tomorrow for
the rest and you can have your bicycle back." The confused
old man was trying to understand why someone wanted his
bicycle and not just natto. The price was far more than he
would make in a week. Thys could wait no longer and
stripped the man of his hat and gently shoved him from the
bicycle. He jumped on the bicycle and pedaled away. Thys
sounded the distinctive natto seller's horn and pulled the
hat low over his head. No one would suspect an old man on
a bicycle. He had a twenty-minute ride to the park to meet
Rie and Peter.

***

As soon as the phone went dead they grabbed their bags, ran from the house and roared off on the bike. Peter wasn't quite sure why they were racing to Thys' place, as they would not be able to help other than to give up the diary. He weaved through traffic but couldn't clear his mind enough to think what to do. Two blocks from the house he pulled over.

"What are you doing? Let's go!"

"No, wait. Let's think this through."

"What? Are you scared? It's my grandparents, come on. You shit!" She slapped him and got off the back of the bike. She ran down the road.

He drove along side her and yelled at her. "Wait. Rie. Wait, think it through."

"You're a coward." He drove the bike onto the sidewalk and blocked her. She tried to get past him but he grabbed her and spun her to face him.

"Is this the face of a coward? Stop and just listen for a second!"

Her eyes pulsed with rage. "What then!" She yelled at him.

"Call them."

"What? Call them? You're an idiot, they need our help."

"Calm down. Call them, see what the situation is. Don't go in there with your kendo sword flying. Think. You have too much passion. Let your brain work. It could be a trap."

She paused for a moment to take in what he was saying. "Yeah, all right." She took out her mobile phone and called. Chieko answered.

"We're fine. Daishin and the boys took a bad beating. I sent Daishin back to the beya. He must fight in the basho this afternoon."

"Of course. You and grandpa are all right?"

"I'm fine just shook up. I'm not as fast as I used to be with the shinai, but I still caused some damage. Daishin looks like Peter."

"Oh no. Can he enter the ring looking like that?"

"I don't know. I'll make a few calls. You must go to Ueno and meet Thys."

"Yes, right away. Do the ultras know where he is?"

"They might. I also think the yakuza had a few cars outside and followed them."

"Oh my God."

"I have phoned my older brother and they are sending two men down to look after Thys. They will meet him at the Taiyaki stand. He knows them."

"Two! Don't we need like twenty?"

"No, these two should be adequate."

Rie hung up the phone and looked ready to cry. She took a deep breath and turned away from Peter. Peter remembered that Chieko said she had only ever seen her cry once. He was about to reach for her when she turned and quickly got back on the rear of the scooter.

"You were right. Let's go to Ueno Park. I know where to meet him."

"Is your grandmother okay?"

"She's fine."

"And Daishin?" There was a pause and he could feel her stomach take a breath behind him. She leaned in and spoke into his ear. Her voice was soft, tightly controlled.

"He'll be fine. We must hurry. Please Peter." Peter wondered about the frailty in her voice. Was it Daishin who she referred to when she spoke of a sumo husband? Maybe there was more than he thought between them. In any case it didn't matter, she didn't show the least encouragement toward him, so he should drop the whole idea. There were more important things at hand.

He pulled away toward Ueno Park.

***

THYS ROLLED up to the taiyaki stand and waited facing away from the crowd. He surveyed the area, there were no ultra nationalists, police or yakuza in the area. There was a tap on his shoulder and he jumped back.

"Hello, sensei."

"Hello, how are you? It has been a few years since we met. Are you well?"

"Yes, sensei. We have been asked to watch over you by the family. We will be nearby."

"Ah my wife. She is everywhere that woman. She is well?"

"Fine and Daishin should compete this afternoon."

The two men, in their twenties, dressed inconspicuously in baggy trousers and dress shirts, were unnoticeable among the crowd. Only if you looked at their feet would you think it odd that they wore old-fashioned tabi shoes, similar to a carpenter's one-toed boots. They had escorted Thys once before when there was some violent reactions about his stand against the yakuza. Highly trained in multiple martial arts they were ruthless and loyal to the Ashikagas. He rested assured there was nothing to fear from

Morinaga. "I was going to buy some taiyaki may I get some for you?"

"No, thank you, sensei. We are nearby should you need us."

"Thank you." The two men drifted away. Thys tipped the sugegasa hat back and the salesman at the stand laughed with delight.

"Ah sensei, you finally got a decent job I see."

"Yes, well, it's about time."

"I hope you and your lovely wife will not be competition for me."

"There is no competition for your treats. May I have three please?"

"Of course." He paid the vendor and bid him farewell. He could see no sign of Peter. He drifted toward the statue of Saigo Takamori. He could see the Taiyaki stand from there and it would be easy to spot Peter and Rie.

The statue loomed over Thys like a scowling guard. Saigo was one of the great heroes of Japanese history and Thys had done extensive research on him when trying to understand the culture of Japan. The concept of the failed hero, so vital to Japanese thought, was an aspect Westerners struggled with. It surprised him, as the 'Charge of the Light Brigade' was not dissimilar, perhaps in fore knowledge of its futility, but certainly not in valor. To give your life in pursuit of an honor-bound, doomed cause was the greatest act of heroism in Japanese lore. Even Saigo, trapped by honor, was isolated on the wrong side and was destined to fight the very government he put in place. The pathos of the paradox that Japanese heroes inevitably find themselves in and which defines them, is a contradiction to worshipping the western conquering hero. He touched the rotund calf of Saigo's leg and peered up at his famous bulbous eyes. Where would the content of Hirohito's diary take him? A group of elderly women were bustling across to a chrysanthemum display on the far side of the park. There were many people heading in that direction. He would have to make a note of taking Chieko there. She did love chrysanthemums.

PETER'S LANGUID gate strode into view behind the sharp staccato struts of Rie. She spoke to the vendor who pointed toward Thys. They headed toward him. He would wait. The much photographed statue, which was controversially left standing by the occupation forces, was in the open and anyone approaching would have to be very blatant.

"Grandpa you're okay." Rie rushed to hug him.

"Yes, yes. Have you spoken—"

"She's fine. Daishin is not so good."

"He was very brave. He took a terrible beating," Thys said.

"She sent him to the basho to contest his bout."

"Excellent. That's as it should be." The old man's smile was enormous. He was not overly disturbed by the drama of the attacks forced upon him. "So shall we have a peak at this book that is causing all this trouble?"

Peter looked around. "Is this a good place? It's a bit open."

"We can see them coming; if they're coming. Did anyone follow you?"

"I don't think so."

"Grandmother said they heard you speaking to us on the phone about Ueno."

"Well, it's a big area. And unless they know of the famous Taiyaki here, we're okay." He held out his hand for the diary. Peter removed his backpack and saw a man watching him. He looked to the other side and saw another man watching.

"Thys, there are two men watching us, one on either side." Rie stepped in closer to Peter. "They look like Yakuza."

Thys chuckled. "They're not yakuza. Yakuza wet themselves when they see these guys. They are on our side. They are 'friends' of Chieko's family."

"Really. They look slimy," Rie said.

"Dangerously so. The pages you gave me were from early on. I think it is important I read the last few weeks first, in case there are things I need to do." Not having anywhere to store the book he tucked it into his haramaki. "It'll be safe in here." Thys had taken to wearing the stomach support band, haramaki, so typical of older Japanese men, years ago. Peter knew that the vital center of man, in Japan, is believed to be located at its gravitational center, the stomach, so it must be supported. The stomach or hara is seen as the container of soul or spirit for the Japanese, not the heart or head, as it is in the West. Hence the whole concept of hara-kiri as the ultimate expression of strength and grief. Peter thought it interesting that the emperor's last thoughts were held so close to Thys' soul. Perhaps Thys Rasmussen really was more Japanese than the Japanese.

As the book slipped in, Thys thought it felt warm and safe.

There was a scrape of gravel behind them to the left and they turned to see one of Chieko's friends standing immediately behind them. The other was to the right. They approached calmly and ushered them further into the park, along the path.

Peter glanced behind him and could immediately see why they had begun to move. A dozen black clad Yakuza youths were making their way toward them. Several of them looked to be carrying short batons or rods at their sides. They approached directly down the path at a steady pace.

One of the friends spoke abruptly. "We need space to fight and an exit point for you. We move toward the other side of the park." Rie started to run. "Don't run. We are in control." Chieko's friends were like ice. They had no emotion, no personality, only intent. Peter was mildly reassured, but still worried as the group closed on them. He could handle two maybe; Rie could handle one, that left nine for the other two 'friends'. They might be all right. *It would be better if Rie had her kendo sword. Where is a demon when you need one?* he thought.

The pursuit continued for two hundred yards, with the yakuza closing steadily. Thys was beginning to breathe heavily, the pace was a bit too strong for him.

Rie glanced across the park. "Oh shit!"

Just to their left another group appeared from the trees at a much faster pace. Right out in the front of the group was Morinaga with the bandaged face of Shimoda beside him. There were about a dozen of them and they obviously wanted first pickings. The Yakuza ran to close the distance.

"Run fifty yards then turn, we must be out in front of both parties to fight," the friend yelled. Rie and Peter each grabbed an arm and hurried Thys along. He wasn't doing well and both parties were closing.

After a moment Morinaga screamed, "You've got no where to run just give it to us. It belongs to the police."

The yakuza closing from the left barked back. "Police my ass! He's an idiot. Give it to us!" The Yakuza made a rush and then the group of ten ultras ran at them, too.

"All right. Now," said one of the friends and they slipped from Peter's view. Peter and Rie continued running with

Thys. The two friends had stopped and made their stand to stop the marauding crowd. They were frightening to watch. They dished out punishment like it was a Bruce Lee movie. Several yakuza were already down with broken arms, unconscious or shattered kneecaps. Shimoda made a run to circle around them to get to Thys. Peter let Rie and Thys go and ran straight back at Shimoda. Shimoda knew Peter wasn't trained in fighting, but what he didn't know was that Peter really hated Shimoda's guts. Peter ran straight into Shimoda's punch but because of his height the blow glanced off his shoulder and his long arms had Shimoda's neck. Using his body and momentum as leverage, he hurled Shimoda high in the air. He slammed down hard on his back. Peter jumped on the winded Shimoda and pummeled him several times knocking the bandages clear from his face. He was unconscious and still Peter pounded him.

"Move, idiot." It was one of the friends who had backed up fighting as he went. Peter scrambled back and saw a man pulling at Rie. He sprinted toward them. Thys was trying to get the man's hands off Rie. Peter struck the man full force with a punch to his solar plexus and the man crumpled gasping for air.

"Run for the exhibit over there. Stay there and hide. I'll come later!" Peter yelled.

Rie and Thys headed off. Peter ran back to the two struggling friends. The numbers were now about ten to three and though the friends were tiring, so too were the attackers. Peter threw himself into the fray. The Yakuza had all but scattered, it was just Morinaga and his morons. One of the 'friends' split Morinaga's mouth wide open with a kick and he spun backwards holding his face. Peter wasn't sure what happened after that, he had his hands full with a flurry of feet, he was trying to smother to get at his attacker's face.

One of his punches landed square on the attacker's ear and must've shattered his eardrum, as the man squealed and stumbled away.

Morinaga's voice sputtered over the crowd. "The van; back to the van, regroup at the van." He and his six remaining men struggled back up the path. Peter was amazed at how far the fight had traveled. There were injured bodies scattered for three hundred yards up the path. Two limp bodies were being carried away. Peter was not sure if they were dead or just unconscious. He wasn't sure he cared. He had never experienced that kind of animal blood rush before.

He turned to see the two 'friends' from hell, bowing to each other and chatting quietly. He wasn't sure what to say. Anything would be appropriate he thought. He approached them slowly. "Thank you. You saved us. We are grateful. I, I've never seen that kind of thing."

"No problem. We are at your service. Where is sensei?" One of them asked. His teeth were crimson, but he didn't seem to notice.

"They will come back we must locate him." The other said as he limped to them. He had taken several shots to the face and his leg was obviously giving him excruciating pain. Peter recalled seeing him hit from behind in the same leg three times with what looked like an iron rod by the yakuza gang. Peter thought that his leg should be broken but knowing these two they wouldn't acknowledge it.

"I told them to hide in the flower exhibit."

"You go in there and stay with them. We will watch out here and if we come inside then we have a problem, but for now the sensei must rest. We need a few moments to gather ourselves."

"Sure. Thank you again. You're a blessing." They

extended their hands to shake. It was then that he noticed their hands were completely red with blood well past the wrist. His hand was shaking madly and he grabbed theirs to hide the embarrassment.

"You're not too bad either. But your arms are too long," one 'friend' said.

"He has an unusual technique – like a giraffe," said the other with the bad leg.

"Yeah, the technique is called panic," Peter said. The 'friends' laughed, one revealed his scarlet mouth. Two teeth were gone on the left side and a massive split opened up when he grinned. He was oblivious to the pain.

***

RIE WAS STANDING on the left side of the exhibit. It was a wide rectangular area about one hundred yards long with the chrysanthemums in tented areas on either side of a central pond. Many visitors, most of them elderly, were milling amongst the flowers taking photos and chatting. As he passed the conversation stopped as startled onlookers gazed at the bloodied disheveled foreigner.

She saw him coming and moved to him. She draped herself against his body. He was shocked. She held him tight. His mind stopped working briefly. She felt like magic. He gazed around the garden. The tranquility was absurd. Minutes before, a few hundred yards up the path, away from the tented area, men were pummeling each other to death, with the 'two ninjas from hell' doing their thing, and here, everyone was chatting about the petals.

"Thank God you're okay." She looked at him. "Damn another split on the lip. No girl will ever want to kiss those sweet lips now."

"You think? I was thinking of only one." He wiped at the blood on his mouth.

"God, your hands." He hadn't noticed but all the skin was gone from his knuckles and they were also spattered with blood. His jaw ached.

"Where is Thys?"

"He is hidden on the far side amongst some matting. He's reading the diary."

"You're okay."

"Yeah, yeah, we both are, thanks to you."

"Hardly, it was the Bruce Lee twins. Those two are totally dangerous."

"Where are they?"

"No idea. They were going to stand watch outside. Let things calm down. They think Morinaga will come back. The Yakuza are history though."

"Let's get a glass of tea." They moved to a small serving area and the apron-clad, old woman looked at him with fear. Her hands shook as she poured the complimentary tea into paper cups. He was about to take it when Rie shot her hands out to take the cups and avoid the sight of his bloody hands. "Let's sit over there on the edge of the pond where we can watch him."

"Did you talk to him at all?" Peter asked.

"No. I walked past once, just before you came. He was shaking slightly. He was upset by what he was reading."

"Your grandmother said they were good friends. Must be hard to be the friend of an Emperor."

"Everyone needs a little kindness." She had no idea why she said it. It rushed out of her heart like a hand snatching at a falling leaf. Was that what her hopes had become? A tear welled in her eye. No, she would snatch harder.

"Not Shimoda." He tried to sip the tea but his hand was shaking violently. He lowered it so as not to be embarrassed. She took it from him and held it to his swollen lips. He took the cup back. "It's okay, I can do it."

"You beat the shit out of Shimoda."

"I had my issues with him." They both looked toward Thys. They could just see the peak of his reed hat. They fell silent. She rubbed his back with a warmth and affection that hazed his mind, blotting out the anger of minutes before. He felt himself calming.

"Please don't get hurt, Peter." She was near tears. "I really couldn't bear to see you beat up any more. If we go to the jazz bar again, they'll think I did it." She tried to laugh it off but really wanted the chance to be with him again. It would end differently.

Peter smiled. "The jazz bar would be nice. Anything other than another round beside the Bruce Lee twins."

***

THYS WAS NOT CALM. There was no calm coming from his reading. It was as if his old friend had suddenly turned, while they were sitting on the shoreline in Iwakuni years before, and spoke to him. He remembered the introverted slight man clearly as if he was sitting on the rock right in front of him. Hirohito had a gentle voice. It was never demanding, never imposing. His voice, which was slightly high, a requirement for a being perceived as a god, drifted off the page in a melancholy fashion. Hirohito, whose position was seen as the embodiment of all that was the art, truth and purity of the bushido way, sat before him in this book. He was the religious and spiritual essence of the people. He was their essence. He was here with his gentle voice speaking among the chrysanthemums. He glanced at the lush flowers surrounding him like nodding spirits. Thys' mind flashed back to his wife and Daishin. Their thoughts were of saving the book, saving these words from their Emperor. Their reverence for the Emperor's words eclipsed courage. They were in a way, protecting their own essence. Daishin with his beaten bloodied face had raged on, while Chieko relished the pride in giving her fighting spirit for this cause, for these final words of a beaten soul. Her battle was the pride of her family, a relish, an honor never stained.

Thys looked back at the words to find the man he knew.

The words were candid and with a purity of thought and obligation. The Emperor was not a politically savvy schemer. He was a man of simple honesty, perhaps naiveté and truth, in the true Bushido spirit.

Stillness enshrouded Thys and Hirohito as they had their last conversation together. It was along entry and Thys drifted languidly over it.

His final words echoed in Thys ears.

'THERE WILL BE no blush on the cherry blossoms that fall across my spirit. They shall all be soiled.'

THE DIARY SLIPPED CLOSED in his palms. There were no more entries. Thys closed his eyes, lost in the impassioned thoughts of a friend he could not reach.

***

RIE AND PETER were at the far end of the long line of chrysanthemums. There had been no disturbance for half an hour and Thys was absorbed by the diary. They approached the corner. There was a break in the tarp that served as a tent backing and a small fire was being tended by one of the gardeners just outside the tented area. The gardener gently prodded the flames.

They had been lulled into a sense of peace by the chrysanthemums and therefore didn't see Morinaga until he was virtually upon them. He must have slipped through the area where the fire was tended. Peter stepped in front of Rie and pushed her through the break in the tent. Morinaga's first punch clipped Peter's jaw and he stumbled backward through the split in the tent. Morinaga, followed by his three thugs, poured through the split.

Peter prepared to fight when a steel poker whisked past his face. Rie had taken it from the stunned gardener. She slashed the glowing red steel across Morinaga's arm, he squealed in pain. She went to strike him again as he struggled to his feet but missed. The 'friends' of Chieko appeared and quickly disposed of the three thugs. Morinaga whirled on Rie and grabbed her throat. He held his pistol to her temple and backed away from the friends and Peter. An idea flashed across Pete's mind and he reached for his bag. He quickly unzipped it.

"I'll kill her if you don't give it to me!" Morinaga screamed.

Peter yanked a book from his bag and waved it wildly. "This is crazy. This should be destroyed."

"No, Peter don't! Don't!" Rie screamed.

Morinaga edged closer to get the book. When he was ten feet away. Peter drew the book back to him and opened it up. He tore the pages from it and madly hurled them into the fire beside him.

"No! No! Peter stop!" Rie screamed and struggled. Morinaga, stunned by the insane action, had his grasp broken and the petite girl broke free.

"No, no you stupid bastard. What've you done!" He pushed Peter backward. Morinaga lunged at the fire and tried to rescue the book. The two friends circled between Rie and Morinaga, who continued to scrabble and attempt to extract the book from the flames. Charcoal pages, like soot-covered butterflies, wafted upward, their edges glowed an innocent orange. Morinaga realized it was useless and spun toward Rie and Peter pointing his revolver toward them.

"You idiot!" The revolver left his hand in an instant and before the gun hit the ground the crack of his arm resounded above the glowing fire. The 'friends' were about to do more damage to the kneeling figure when Rie stepped forward.

"You pathetic son of a bitch!" She kicked his chest and he fell back holding his broken arm. "Leave him to cry over his book." Escorted by the 'friends' they made their way past the three injured thugs, one who was still unconscious, up to where Thys sat in a deeply contemplative mood.

"What was the book?" Rie asked.

"It was my book of kanji practice pages. Two months of writing drills." She laughed. "You caught on really quick."

"Well, maybe I can become your Kanji teacher." He rolled his eyes. Rie pulled herself tight onto his arm.

They arrived near the huddled figure of Thys. Rie went to his side. "Grandpa, are you alright?"

"Yes, perhaps." He glanced up at the dark almond eyes, so kind, so fierce, so proudly Japanese. 'Bushido' he thought. The sight of Chieko's pride and joy as she stood beside the bloodied sumo in a battle against an obscene gaggle of thugs flashed through his mind. Rie possessed the same proud eyes. "Perhaps I have been here too long. Perhaps we have all been here too long."

"What's wrong, what does it say?" she asked. He merely tightened his grip around her arm and with the diary under one arm and his treasured granddaughter wrapped on the other, he ambled toward the exhibition exit. Rie glanced back at Peter. He was a step behind her, his eyes looked only at her. There was an odd lost look in them, as if a small boy was watching a paper boat sink in a stream, both happy and sad. She turned back and squeezed the old man's arm. She could see a small twinge of knowing at the corner of his mouth. They strolled from the garden followed several yards back by the ever-present 'friends'.

Thys, looking much older than before, stopped at the last chrysanthemum arrangement located at the corner of the exhibit near the exit. It was a white sunburst of petals. He released her arm and caressed the underside of the over-flowing petals with the back of his hand. He stroked them as if they were a baby's cheek. "It tells of a man, who as a boy was weak, and only found strength in his failure as a man. As Emperor, he was given a unique choice to end his life in suicide or to bear the humiliation of the nation in order to free his people of shame." His hand pulled away and took her arm again leading her into the vast Ueno Park. "He knew MacArthur sought to not only rid the Japanese of the criminals of the war, that was easy, but he also wanted to castrate the Japanese soul – a far greater, crueler victory. Therefore, he convinced the Emperor to remain in place and nurture the nation. In so doing, Hirohito chose to live a life persecuted by his shame, to atone for the deaths of so many. He chose to survive as the embodiment of failure, hoping that in his penance he would then allow his people to rise up, and regain the bushido spirit, as he spiraled further down. It was, he believed, the ultimate hero's sacrifice, greater than life itself. But sadly he felt he was chastised by fate and saw, instead of his people rise up in their bushido spirit, they sold out to mercantile interests. His heroic sufferance of shame for the nation, instead of being lauded, was debased and trivialized. His greatest gift, greater than his life, was rejected. He was forever a failure never enduring the honored failure of a Japanese hero. Yet to me he has endured a suffering greater than the heroes Kusunoki Masashige or even the great Saigo Takamori. Sadly Hirohito lays buried as a villain to his own and to other peoples memories."

"Honor in life is often a brutal sadness," Peter said solemnly.

The comment caught Thys' thoughts, pulling him away from the diary. "Good God Peter! Such insight and pain from one so young." Thys stared up at the tall gangly Dane whose face was peppered with welts, his eyes black with crimson centers. '*A Dane caught in the Bushido spirit,*' he thought. "But you are right. It can be a brutal life and one which should be ended at the pinnacle, as Yukio Mishima said."

"We should get back to grandmother."

"Yes, Rie." He leaned back slightly to glance at the two

dangerous young guards who were a respectful distance behind. "Will you accompany me home?" They bowed. "Rie, I have an important meeting to attend and some decisions to make. You must watch Daishin fight for his first Kachikochi. It will be a great moment for him." Rie's body stiffened with the thought of not being there for her brother. "It's just about three. If you go straight there, he will get you in. Go now I will call Chieko, she can arrange it."

Peter watched as Rie's eyes burst with expectation; like mercury her passions could swing from extreme to extreme. "We've got to be there. Come on, Pete." She dashed off and then turned and sprinted back. She gave the old man a kiss on his cheek. She ran back to Peter and snatched his arm. They ran for the nearest taxi.

***

THEY ARRIVED late and missed the grand entrance of the sumo but still got a brief nod from Daishin as he passed back to the stables to wait for his bout. An old man appeared at their side. He was clad in a grey hitched up kimono similar to the style the farm workers wore in the fields. He didn't walk he moved at a constant half jog. His grin was a huge eruption of teeth.

"This way quickly it will start soon. There is a reservation for you."

"We should clean up," Rie said.

"I will bring extra Oshibori wash cloths for you, but maybe he needs a new face. I'll bring a tengu mask."

"The nose would be too small," Peter countered.

The old man cackled. "Your Japanese is very good. Daishin said you were very special guests." The toothy grin turned to Peter. "Today though, your two faces; you and Daishin, are like twins."

He waved them to follow him to their seats. They proceeded awkwardly, attempting to keep up with his half jog. It was more of an open cubicle than a seat and was made for four people. It was a simple raised tatami mat with four zabutton cushions to sit on. They were extremely close to the sumo Dojo. The seated area must have cost thousands Peter thought as they were usually retained through generations. No sooner had they settled than the little man reappeared with a tray of sake and beer. He immediately poured for both of them. Peter deftly snatched the one liter bottle from his hand and held a glass for him.

"No, no, no."

"Yes, yes, yes." Peter made a big performance out of the offering and raised this voice. Peter was unaware of his bloodied ghoulish appearance. He was too caught up in the excitement of the tournament. "Come on old sage. We need some inside information. Will Daishin win today? Will he get kachikoshi?"

Several neighboring visitors leaned in for the information. They were intrigued by the bloody foreigner who spoke Japanese and the bouncing beauty beside him. The old man played to the crowd. "Ah. He has missed some fights and he's against a top Ozeki, plus his face is as ugly as yours. I need two tengu masks one with a big nose for the foreigner and one fat one for Daishin." The nearby crowd howled its approval. "But your answer," the old boy had the crowd suspended on his lips, "lies in her heart." He pointed at Rie.

She jumped up. "Then yes. Yes! My brother will win

Kachikoshi!" The crowd cheered the pretty little woman. The old man shuffled off on his duties. Rie explained more of the details of sumo and her history with Daishin to Peter during the preliminary bouts. The neighboring boxes were enthralled when they heard that Daishin was her brother. The truth could always be stretched when it was in support of a good man.

Food poured forth endlessly and there was no way of stopping the energetic beaver of a man. Every cubicle received the same endless treatment. The excitement with each bout grew and infected the crowd. Peter could feel the pulse from the thousands in the specially designed grand sumo hall. All the spectators had their favorites and were living on the edge of their seats with each battle of the big men.

It was one of the last three bouts when Daishin came up and stamped his feet dropping deep into a traditional open kneed squat. He glared at the Ozeki squatting before him. There had been a gasp when Daishin appeared, both his eyes were purple and his body had numerous welts. His lip was split and he had one eyebrow bandaged. The state of his body did not lessen the demeanor of his scowl. Both men needed to get a majority of eight wins out of the fifteen bouts in the tournament and as this was the last day it was all on the line for both men. It was one of the most highly sought after battles of the tournament. It would be Daishin's first Kachikoshi and to take it from an Ozeki, the second highest ranked wrestler, would be a very sweet prize. The salt was hurled high in the air across the sand dojo for the third and final time. The salt, used to appease evil demons, also fired the spirit of anticipation rippling through the crowd. They cheered the men madly. Rie was beside herself with screams. The men went to crouch, head to head, one hand on the sand, the other poised to touch. There was total silence. The Ozeki rocked back, he was not ready. They would have to re-center. They stood and then went into a crouch, again with one fist on the sand of the dojo the other ready to tap it to start. Silence. Daishin rocked back, he was not ready. The crowd howled in anticipation. Rie was about to have a heart attack. They returned to crouch with a single hand poised. SLAM! They hit each other. Throat thrusts lashed from both men as they slashed violently at each other. Daishin slipped to the left and caught the Ozeki's belt with both hands. He immediately squatted and lifted the other behemoth clear of the floor. The opposing four-hundred pounder wriggled and thrashed his legs in a vain attempt to gain a footing as he was marched to the edge of the reed perimeter. Daishin did not throw him down. He instead humiliated the fellow behemoth by setting him gently outside ring. Could there have been a greater victory?

Rie was screaming. Maintaining the austere calm of a sumo he accepted the win and then instead of returning to the dressing room he walked around the dojo, stood directly in front of their box and bowed solemnly to Peter and Rie. Peter returned the bow. Rie just bounced and bounced. The crowd went wild. Daishin returned to the dressing room.

As luck would have it Daishin was chosen to perform the closing ceremony on his first Kachikoshi day. The ornate structured dance with a bow was performed to perfection. Rie cheered and hooted at every traditional sweep of the bow. She was literally orchestrating the crowd's reactions. Daishin smiled and waved to her before leaving. She continued to bounce in utter ecstasy. She was crazy with joy, utterly crazy. Cushions were flying through the air, as was tradition, raining down on the dojo. She hugged Peter as if he might disappear. Suddenly she reached up and kissed him long on the lips. The passion struck him so hard he couldn't respond. There was a tugging at the their legs. She wouldn't release him. The crazy old beaver in the hitched up kimono, who had served the bounty of food, continued to tug.

"Oi. Stop that." The old boy continued to tug at her, but she didn't want to let Peter go. Peter had to finally break away. "Riechan," the toothy grin sputtered, "Daishin has asked you to join him at the beya for a party tonight and you must bring your lover."

"Oh no, he's not my lover." She was shocked at the obvious thought.

"Why not?" the little man asked.

"Yeah, why not?" Peter added turning her back to him.

"Well, for one night, I guess." Her eyes enchanted Peter he could say nothing.

"One night can be a lifetime." The little man chuckled as he jogged away.

Rie turned back to him. Her eyes reached deep into his soul. "I hope it can be a lifetime." Her lips took Peter's gently as she tried to kiss around the wounds.

***

Thys' mind was clearly made up. When he put the call through to the chamberlain to arrange an appointment the chamberlain was already abreast of the situation. He was allowed an audience at six that evening. A car was sent to pick them up and they arrived just before six with the three bonsai trays. Attendants carried the trays from the car and they were personally greeted at the entrance by the chamberlain. Both Chieko and Thys had visited the Palace on numerous occasions but never in a capacity similar to today. Chieko of course wore her formal family kimono with kamon, family crest, displayed. The Ashikagas were not the kind to hide their pride. Chieko's left eye was completely bloodshot and her lip severely swollen. All other bruises had been covered with make up.

The Emperor received them in the garden, which was an informal and respectful observance of the long friendship Thys had had with Emperor Showa.

After the formal greetings the Empress, who was a particular friend of Chieko's, invited her to stroll the gardens. Before she left the Empress turned to Thys. "You must watch Sumo Digest this evening," she said. "You must be very proud of Daishin he is a remarkable young sumo, but also watch the crowd." The Empress glanced at her husband who smiled and nodded. "Your granddaughter Rie is hilarious. I have never seen anyone so enthused about a win."

The Emperor laughed as well. "You would have thought she had won. It was quite a sight. You must be very proud."

"Yes, thank you. I apologize for my granddaughters behavior." Chieko said diplomatically, though she would have done the same thing.

"Apologize? I thought it made the evening." The Emperor laughed again. "Don't let her forget it."

"That's what grandparents are for," Chieko added.

The Empress laughed and she slipped off with Chieko. They were very relaxed in each other's company. Thys thought perhaps it was only himself who felt a burden today. Thys thought the Emperor was in a very relaxed mood. He had not been with the young Emperor for many years and had grown accustomed to the more dower personality of Hirohito.

The Emperor turned his focus to Thys. "Please sit, my father would be appalled if he saw a man of such respect standing." Thys took a seat. The Emperor looked at the three bonsai trays. "So you have had some discoveries and it looks from your eyes they are a weight on your shoulders."

"I have found a diary secreted within the great Showa Emperor's bonsai. I was puzzled why he insisted I tend the bonsai and have been very honored. My field is not familiar with the intricacies of bonsai, he knew that, but I was most honored when he allowed me the privilege."

"I think we both know, had it been left to anyone else, they would not have thrived, though judging from the state of one that is not so." The Emperor rose and Thys also got to his feet. The Emperor crossed down to where the three bonsai had been placed. He examined the Meiji and Taisho bonsai with great fascination. He then moved to the Showa tray touched the base and turned back to face Thys. There was not anger in his eyes, only an expectancy. "So?"

"I have the diary here." Thys was reluctant to give it to the Emperor, which was ridiculous as it was the Emperor's father's diary. Thys just wanted to hold onto it for a few moments longer. The Emperor must have sensed the reluctance and waved him back to the chairs.

"You hold the diary with great respect. My father would have appreciated that. I have heard you and your family have endured many pains to protect the diary."

"They were only small tribulations."

"Hah! Not if you look at Daishin and the young boy. Their faces are not pretty. Even your granddaughter and wife have been injured. I am most sorry for this and deeply respect their efforts."

"Your highness, I must explain my actions towards the Emperor Showa's Bonsai. As you can see it has been destroyed beyond repair. It was burned, this afternoon, very sadly, by me. I watched it go and felt I lost my dear friend Emperor Showa again. The reason is contained within the diary, the later entries asked that it be destroyed. I felt obligated to do as Emperor Showa wished."

"It would not have been an easy task. Emperor Showa was lucky to have had such a friend as you."

"It was my good fortune."

"True friendships are indeed a rare commodity. I believe my father had even fewer than most. He was naturally an introverted man."

"He was a man of great thought, greater than most realize. Please take the book. I believe it is important you read it to explain my actions and his wishes."

"Of course. Should I return it to you? It was after all entrusted to you with the greatest of respect."

"No, please keep it for your family."

"Have you read it?"

Thys considered his answer for a moment. It would be an invasion of anyone's privacy to read another's diary, let alone the Emperor of Japan. He looked at the young Emperor. "Yes. Yes I have, and many tears wet the pages." The Emperor remained silent and studied the older man. Few men had reached his level of respect in the country, whether they were Japanese or not. Thys Rasmussen had in many ways distilled the essence of Japan and drank deeply from the cup.

The Emperor spoke softly, "What do you think I should do with it?"

"It is not for me to say, but I believe the entries should be read by all of your descendants so that they might know the endurance of one man to carry the burden of having lost the soul of the country, as he saw it."

The Emperor straightened slightly. Such a bold statement fifty or a hundred years ago would have assured the speaker of certain death. But Thys Rasmussen was a man of honor and would never utter a word to harm Emperor Showa or the throne. "Tell me, do you believe our modern society has now begun to move forward into a better direction and a more fulfilling world than that of Imperial Japan one hundred years ago?"

"That too is not for me to say. I do believe the answer is within you as leader of this great nation."

The Emperor smiled at the circumspect answer. It was a very Japanese response. "I think we shall take the burden of tending these three bonsai from your shoulders, but we will keep the Showa Emperor's as is; scorched and charred, as one of three. Perhaps you would be good enough to view my own bonsai and that of my children?" The Emperor stood and Thys bowed.

"It would be my pleasure." The young Emperor led the way from the small pavilion. The two men walked past the three bonsai. They paused before the charred remains of Hirohito's, the late Showa Emperor's elm that had survived for more than one hundred years. Now the roots were gnarled black fingers and the charcoal of the tiny bough stood erect, its cleaved trunk stark and barren, withered in the sun. Decades of history, of thoughts, passed through their minds. The spirit of the bonsai, twisted and blackened, encompassed a vast world.

They walked on, leaving the diary at the base of the burned bonsai. The summer wind fluttered the pages and slipped silently through the charcoal branches. The bonsai's spirit was cast fleetingly upon the wind.

9

EPILOGUE... A DIARY ENTRY

From the Author,
I hope you have enjoyed this adventure.
It has been intended as a means to explore
Tokyo and the evolving culture of a fascinating island at the
turn of the century.

To keep the atmosphere of this book in the light I had
intended, I have moved the final entry to my website.

I initially had taken the position that it should be
included within the book but in truth it added a different
dimension and finished the book with a different energy,
much more solemn.

I therefore ask you, if your interest is there, to go to my
website and peruse, what I think, may be a last entry by a
man who led his nation for six decades.

There is no log in, no email address required, none of
that, I just suggest a slow read of the brief essay. Right or
wrong it lends a different aspect to the sun that has set on
Emperor Showa.

.   .   .

"THERE WILL BE no blush on the cherry blossoms that fall across my spirit. They shall all be soiled."

FEEDBACK AND CONTACT

Other works and grateful feedback.

If you wish to contact me regarding your thoughts on the novel or about any of my novels I am always grateful. We can only enhance our worlds through understanding and communication. My author website www. kfarranauthor.com

If you have time to leave a review, however brief, it would be immensely appreciated by me and other readers. Hearing the thoughts of others enriches all of us and fuels the neurones that make us unique.

If you would like to order any of my other novels please find me on the various platforms or go to my website where I offer various box sets/novels and info on my literary journey. You can find me on instagram or facebook also.

Thank you again for sharing your time to read my novel and I hope it was rewarding. Until we meet on a literary adventure again, I wish you well.

Sincerely,

Kevin

ABOUT THE AUTHOR

Hi, thank you for venturing onto my small patch of beach, where I am but one grain of sand among billions of others on our tiny planet.

I am a lover of Great Danes, road cycling, and classic cars. I split my time between solitary literary pursuits, working with my designer wife on home restorations and supporting our son's football careers.

I am a wanderer. My boys and lovely partner of more than three decades, have been dragged from one adventure to another. Much in the same way I was as a youth. I was born in Barotseland formerly part of Northern Rhodesia and now a reluctant part of Zambia. Through many countries in North America , the Orient and Europe I have now (temporarily) come to rest in Spain.

When wandering, a vast array of abilities becomes stowed in one's baggage, my rumpled duffle bag is no different. From performing Shakespeare and Tennessee Williams, to teaching and heavy equipment operation, even to pig and dairy farms, high-end restaurants and period home renovation, all add spice to the dish that is me.

(One thinks too many chefs ruin the dish?)

Perhaps – it is what it is.

I dwell in possibility.

That is why I love to engage stories and explore what might 'be'.

I hope you enjoy the journey, we are all in search of

'the great perhaps.'

For more information
www.kfarranauthor.com
kfarranauthor@gmail.com

ALSO BY KEVIN FARRAN

Taemane

The beauty of greed crashes into the brutality of diamonds in 1950 South Africa. Two sisters battle to control their loves and lives as their inherited diamond mind comes under attack. Taemane

The Bench

Jenny the highly educated office mouse has her passions torn asunder and laid bare by the chance discovery of a lover's poem, and then another, and another.

Is this a delusion or is love transforming her?

The Bench

Beyond Charitable Lines

Saddled with doo-gooders and the snivelling press, Thomas fights an outbreak of the disfiguring disease NOMA in Sudan's rebel territories. One man's attempt to save the desperate refugees on his doorstep.

A triumph for survival and hope against man and disease. Beyond Charitable Lines

Strokes of Deceit

Two brothers, divergent in character, but unified by one love, embark on a journey neither is likely to return from. When a moment of madness, self-preservation or all consuming love leads to a fateful decision, it divides them ensuring that honour and deceit destroy the purity of love.

Strokes of Deceit

The Chocolate Fix

Personal tragedies toss four women into a mix of mud-packs, masks and madness that leads to an exfoliation of the spirit that is both gory and gregarious.

A sisterhood in chocolate.

The Chocolate Fix

Bathe Me

The power of a child's dream... even if it's a lie.

Outcast on the streets of Uganda, two orphans survive a nightmare existence to pursue a childhood dream.

Bathe Me

Hidden

Nature vs Nurture

An unsuspecting New York abstract sculptor is entwined with a beautiful German journalist who reveals a repulsive past they never knew, and they genetically cannot escape from. Escaping that past may cost them their lives.

The only need to solve one question, but as the offspring of the world's greatest sociopath — can they?

Hidden

Kiss of the Kris

A young girl's journey from terrorist to pacifist. Imprisoned for four years, Celeste escapes to become the leader of the resistance in a struggle to stop the programmed annihilation of her people by... themselves.

Kiss of the Kris

The Searching

Deceived and distrusted by his family's country of choice, Kenichi Sugano rejects the spartan Japanese internment prison inflicted on his family by America, to endure the death fields of Europe, and the smoking staggering corpse that is Tokyo. Nurtured by the true hearts of brave women and the steaming bloody hearts of dying friends, he searches to find love, honor and a sense of identity.

The Searching

I Love You, I'm Sorry. I'm Sorry, I love You

Five simple words explored in five novellas. How many different meanings can these lines contain. Five eras, five countries, five stories all finishing on the same five words.

An exploration of love.

I Love You, I'm Sorry

Heart of Stone

Designed for the beauty of the female voice, Barcelona's most beautiful building harbours an ugly screaming truth of tragic love. American architect Ignacio Thomas is captivated and consumed by two great beauties - one flesh and bone, the other bricks and mortar. Equally enticing, both possess haunting pasts and alluring futures.

Heart of Stone

COMING SOON BY KEVIN FARRAN

Made in the USA
Columbia, SC
02 June 2023